D1343837

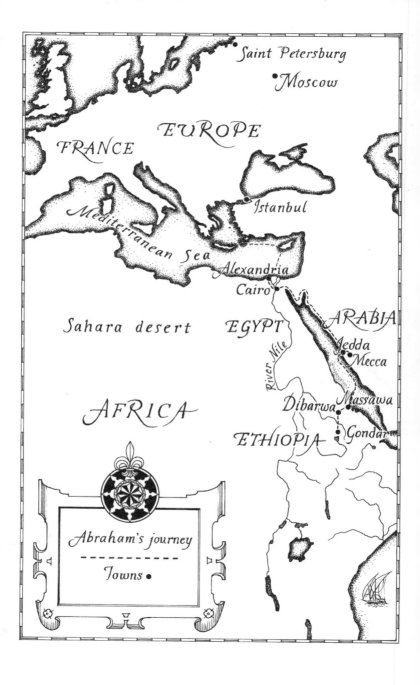

For Nina
with love from

ABRAHAM
HANNIBAL
and the Raiders of the Sands

Frances Somers Cocks

FRANCES SOMERS COCKS
ILLUSTRATED BY ERIC ROBSON

First published in Great Britain in 2003 by the Goldhawk Press
19 Kempson Road, London SW6 4PX
email goldhawkpress@btopenworld.com

Produced for the Goldhawk Press by
Umberto Allemandi & C., Turin ~ London ~ Venice

Printed and bound in Italy

ISBN 0 9544034 0 1

British Library Cataloguing-in-Publication Data: a catalogue record
for this book is available from the British Library

*The front cover illustration, by Eric Robson, shows Abraham
in the robes of a deacon of the Ethiopian Orthodox Church.*

for Abraham Alexander
- his book

ABOUT THE AUTHOR

Frances Somers Cocks has been a teacher in England, Africa, Spain and China. This has been handy, because she has been able to use the school holidays to go travelling in Abraham Hannibal's footsteps and to research and write his story. Her journeys have been by bus, lorry, camel, train and boat, and have mostly been uncomfortable but good fun. She has never been shipwrecked or captured by pirates, though she did get into terrible trouble with her head-teacher once, when her boat got stuck in the Red Sea and she got back to school two weeks late (not that the children were bothered!)

Frances Somers Cocks lives in London with her son Abraham Alexander and a ginger tom-cat called Nimrod, in a messy flat full of weird and lovely pictures, carvings and ornaments from all over the world – but especially from the countries where Abraham Hannibal lived.

CONTENTS

THE RED SEA, ARABIA
& THE MEDITERRANEAN
1704

GLOSSARY AND GUIDE
TO PRONUNCIATION

Abba Mikail (say MICK-a-eel) Father Mikail,
    an old monk or holy man
caravan a large group of travellers or traders and
    their horses, mules, donkeys or camels
dhow a traditional Arab sailing-boat, with only one
    mast and sail
Doctor Poncet (say PON-say) a French doctor
    to the Ethiopian Emperor
Fares (say FAR-res) Abraham's father,
    a prince known as the Lord of the Sea
fast give up meat, milk and eggs
Frank a white person, a person from northern
    Europe; a French person
Holy of Holies the most important, secret part
    of an Ethiopian church
Lahia (say La-HEE-a) Abraham's older sister,
    his only full sister
Makeda (say Ma-KAY-da) Abraham's mother;
    also the Queen of Sheba in the Bible
mule a cross between a donkey and a horse
pilgrimage a journey to a holy place
Ras of Tigre (say TEE-gray) Prince of Tigre,
    in the north-eastern part of Ethiopia
teff the most common grain grown in Ethiopia,
    used for making giant pancakes

Chapter 1

STAMPEDE!

The boy heard the elephants long before he saw them. The cows he was supposed to be looking after were looking after themselves very well, and his brothers had all disappeared. It was the dead time of the afternoon, and the air was heavy and very hot, but he was wide-awake. He crouched in the damp red earth under the old thorn-tree on the King's Hill, his white cotton breeches thick with red dust, carefully placing the last stalks of grass on the roof of a tiny hut. The other herd-boys sometimes made little cows out of clay, but he'd grown out of those long ago. Buildings were what *he* liked to make: houses and churches and sometimes great fantastical castles that fell down before he could finish what was in his mind's eye.

"*There*'s the cooking hut," he whispered to himself. "And *this* is Father's palace. *Here* is our hut. I won't do all of the huts. Let's see. Church next, or wall?" He chewed his muddy fingernails and thought. Then he picked up a branch and scraped a rough circle round the little settlement, scooped up a handful of earth, and started shaping a yard-wall.

Then he heard it - and felt it: first, his cows shifting and mooing uneasily, then branches crashing and splintering, the shudder of the ground under his bare feet, and the terrible groaning bray of an elephant in pain. He bolted up out of the shade and looked down around him. From the Wild Lands of the west came tramping steadily through the scrub three dozen or more elephants - cows, a few young bulls, and babies.

ELEPHANTS! Here? Up in the highlands? He'd never heard of such a thing! He cried out in delight, "Hey! You! You! What are *you* doing here?"

And then suddenly, Abraham saw what the elephants had seen: the fields that edged the town, the delicious young shoots of *teff-*

grain, the tender seedlings of beans and oil-nuts. And just on the other side of the fields lay the first of the rough stone and mud houses of his father's capital - Dibarwa. The herd's leader gave a great bellow, the babies squealed, and the whole troop broke into a heavy blundering charge towards the crops.

They've got to be stopped ... They've got to be stopped ... I have to stop them ...

Abraham hardly knew what he had in mind, but he found himself racing down from his little hill and across the meadows to get in ahead of the trampling feet, between them and his town, between the trampling feet and the harvest, between the trampling feet and the little children and the grey-beards dozing in the yards. He could hear himself screaming, "THIS WAY! THIS WAY!"

And then he was right in front of them, running half-sideways, pulling off his white cotton cloak and flapping it wildly, then grubbing up stones as he ran and flinging them at the herd, *willing* them towards him and away from his town. He could see that at the head of the crazed army was an old she-elephant, bellowing with pain and fury, her face oozing and puffy where a spear had stuck in her right cheek.

Abraham dodged away from the town towards the steep red banks of the Mareb river, and the old elephant swerved after him, thundering ever nearer; obediently the army wheeled towards the river too. The boy stumbled on and on across the stony soil, gasping fiercely.

Until suddenly he was falling through space.

Chapter 2

SON OF THE LORD OF THE SEA

Slowly Abraham opened his eyes, but he closed them again straight away. His head hurt terribly, and he felt stiff and sore all over.

"My son? My son? Can you hear me?"
It was the voice of his mother, Makeda. He tried opening his eyes again; thank goodness the light was very dim. They were in his mother's hut. She was bending over him, very close, wiping his forehead with a wet cloth. He wasn't lying on his usual cow-skin on the floor, but actually up on the clay bed.

"What happened with the elephants?" he whispered.

"You fell into the Mareb, and the old leader fell in right after you. She was sick - the pain in her face must have driven her mad, to make her stray so far from home. She fell all the way down to the river-bed. What a young hot-head you are!"

Smiling down at him, his mother fingered the silver cross that he had worn on a string round his neck since he was christened at forty days old.

"Someone in Heaven must have been looking after you: you landed on a bushy ledge a little way down. When the herd saw their leader dead, they lost courage, and soon headed away, back down towards the Wild Lands. Some of your brothers saw it all. You were very brave."

"Does Father know?"

"He knows. He was here when you were unconscious. He'll be back soon. He's very proud of you."

Abraham smiled and then whispered, "What about Lahia?"

"I'm here," said his sister's voice, and she came up out of the shadows. "Little brother, I thought I had lost you. Thank God and Our Lady that you are safe." And she knelt on the bed to hug him. Lahia – Beauty - lived up to her name: like her brother and her mother, she was very dark-skinned, and she was often teased for it, but no-one could tease her for her huge dark eyes, her smooth oval face, and her ready, cheerful smile. Her mother's hair would never grow quite long enough to bush out properly at the ends of the braids she wore plaited back along her head, but Lahia looked a real young lady, with *her* plaits ending in a lovely black cloud that floated at the back of her neck.

That night Abraham lay restless and sweating in the chilly winter air, unable to sleep. Rain dripped through the gaps in the grass roof.

Why hasn't Father come yet? Why hasn't he come? Why hasn't he come?

"Mother?"

"My son?"

"Tell me the story again."

"Which story?" smiled his mother, although she knew.

"Of how Father met you."

She came and sat next to him, and

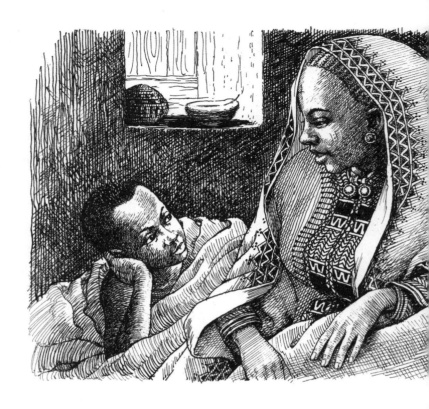

wrapped them both up in her white cloak, and Lahia sat at the end of the bed and listened too.

"Long ago, in days long gone by, the Lord of the Sea was hunting down in the Wild Lands, where it is hot as the Devil's home and men do not know Jesus and the saints. It was a mighty hunt. The spears of the Lord of the Sea and his warriors dripped with blood. They came upon a great herd of elephants, and

many were the tusks of ivory they carried off
that day. Leopards were slain in plenty; now
their skins adorn the shoulders of the brave. A
score of lions died, and the mightiest princes
in the land now wear their manes. And they
hunted my people too: twenty-eight children
of the Kunama, the Slave-People, were taken
from my own village, near where the waters of
the Mareb begin to die in the dryness of the
plains."

Abraham Hannibal

"Sing us the children's song, Mother."

And Makeda sang the sorrowful song of the children of her people:

"They come and catch us by the waters of
                    the Mareb
They make us slaves.
Our mothers in fear flee to the mountains,
And leave us alone in strange hands ..."

Makeda's voice began to tremble, and she stopped. The three of them stayed silent a moment, and then she went on with the tale.

"The warriors fell on our village like a thundercloud. What a screaming and wailing there was, what a rushing into the hills! Men and women ran to save themselves, and the slowest and the youngest were caught. They were rounded up with whips and their hands tied with ropes. Only the old folk were left. One girl hid in a pile of firewood, pulled an old skin over her head, and peeped out from under it. Then she saw one man who had not fled. It was her father. Slowly, silently, with a knife in his hand, he was creeping through the

shadows, through the trees round our village, to where the Lord of the Sea stood and watched his warriors collect their booty."

"My father?" said Abraham, although he knew.

His mother nodded. "Suddenly, the girl's father dashed out of the shadows and lunged at the Lord. But he was too slow. The Lord of the Sea swung round, smashed the knife out of his hand, and tripped him to the ground. He stood over the body, placed one foot on his chest, and raised his spear high ...

"Then, from out of the woodpile burst the girl; she ran across the clearing and, with a great cry of '*STOP!*' she threw herself over the body of her father. She twisted round to look up at the spear that pointed at her throat, and saw the face of her enemy looking down at her. The sharp point wavered; the enemy stepped back. The Lord of the Sea up-ended his spear and stuck the handle in the earth.

"'Stand up!' he commanded. The girl and her father rose, trembling.

"'Is this your daughter?' asked the Lord of the Sea.

"The Kunama looked him straight in the eyes. 'She is.'

"'You are to go free. But your daughter is to become my wife. She will be treated with honour.'

"And so the girl left the Wild Lands for ever, and lived on the high tableland, in the land of the Christians. She was christened with the name of Makeda, and she became the youngest of the wives of the Lord of the Sea."

"And they had a wise and lovely daughter called Lahia, and a crazy, brave boy called Abraham, and they all lived happily ever after ..." chanted Lahia, with a sparkle in her eyes. But her brother was breathing evenly now, ready for sleep ...

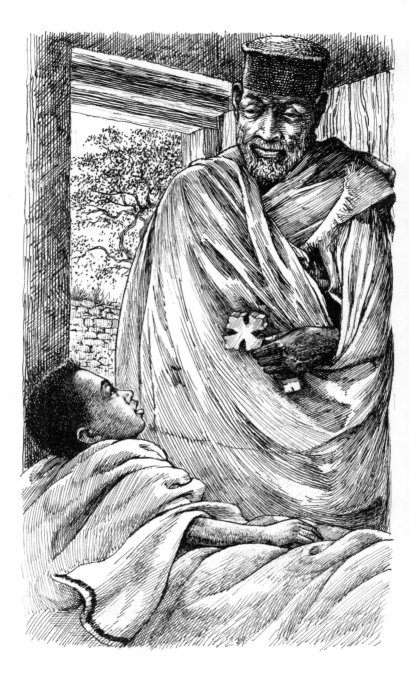

Chapter 3

THE OLD MONK

The next morning he woke to find a visitor sitting on his bed, a tall old man in yellow robe and cap.

"Abba Mikail!" cried Abraham.

The old monk smiled.

"I see we will soon have you back at class. We've missed you, you know. You keep the other boys on their toes."

It was true that Abraham was Abba Mikail's liveliest pupil. It wasn't that he found the classes easy - it was hard to say which was worse: learning the Bible off by heart in the strange old language of the church that he could hardly understand, or coming to grips with the alphabet. About the only advantage that Abraham could see to being a girl was that girls didn't have to go to school.

Abraham Hannibal

The alphabet drove him and the other boys mad. Two hundred and seventy-odd letters to learn and practise: *ha, hoo, hee, ta, too, tee, ba, boo, bee*, and so on, endlessly.

If Abraham did well, Abba Mikail let him look at his most precious book, *Stories of the Kings*, which had pictures in it, and showed him how to draw some of the people on spare scraps of skin. There was King Solomon on his throne - King Solomon, the Lion of the Tribe

of Judah - and Makeda, the Queen of Sheba, in robes of red and gold, with a great line of her camels and slaves bringing the king all the riches of her land: gold and spices and precious stones. Abraham knew the whole story, and he loved it; after all, his own mother was called after the Queen of Sheba. Some bits of the story were in the Bible too; it was an old, old tale.

When Abba Mikail was in an easy-going mood, he would gather the boys round and tell them how Makeda, a great queen in Ethiopia in ages long gone by, went to visit Solomon, king of the Jews, just as it said in the Bible, and how they loved each other; and how they had a son called Menelik, who became the first Ethiopian King of Kings, and the forefather of their Emperor. And Abraham and his brothers would sit a little prouder, since they knew that their father, on Granny Ester's side, was also of the line of Solomon and Menelik.

"We'll have you back with your pens and your colours in no time. You're turning into a real little monk, you know. Maybe you'll become one."

"That's what Father calls me: 'little monk'. But I don't know. Monks aren't allowed to hunt or fight, are they? And they wouldn't get to do much riding. I think I'd miss that. I think I'd just like to be a warrior who draws pictures."

He stopped, and made a face.

"Sorry, Abba Mikail. My head's suddenly hurting again."

"You're a brave boy, and a bright one too."

And in the strange old language of the church, Abba Mikail blessed him. He stayed till the boy was asleep, and then he went down the slope to his little room in a tower by Saint Mary's church.

Chapter 4

THE LORD OF THE SEA
RETURNS

The next afternoon, Lahia helped Abraham out of the hut. They walked slowly, arm-in-arm, across the muddy yard with its rough stone palace the only two-storey building, and a scattering of huts for cooking and brewing and storage, huts for wives and for slaves. They made their way through the chickens and the new lambs, the clutter of cooking pots and water pots and beer pots, of grinding stones and grain-baskets and water-skins. Many people were still out of the compound on their different duties, but every-one who was there, all the children - their half-sisters and half-brothers - and the house-slaves, all of them cheered and clapped. The women-folk, including Granny Ester (his father's

mother), and Makeda, and his father's seven
other wives, gave their ear-splitting trill of joy.

Even Abraham's two least favourite stepmothers, who had a habit of making pointed
remarks about slaves and the Kunama and
people with dark skins when he or his mother
or sister were in earshot, joined in the congra-
tulations.

Abraham blinked and bit his lips with
happiness.

Not bad, for the youngest boy! Not bad for a grandson of the Kunama, the Slave-People!

Very, very carefully, the two children clambered up the huge rough stones of the yard wall, sat themselves on the top, and look-ed around them. Below them the hillside fell steeply down to the plain: the royal compound lay at the end of a high, narrow ridge - Saint Mary's Hill - and on two of its sides there was a sheer drop. On the third side was a gradual slope down to the church of Saint Mary, and on the fourth, the steep path down to the town.

Round most of the bottom of the hill swarmed Dibarwa, his father's capital, a town of long low stone-and-mud houses with heavy flat roofs, here and there a thatched round hut, all crowded together higgledy-piggledy, the alley-ways and the yards and even the roofs bright green with wild plants at this time of the Big Rains.

The town stretched right across from Saint Mary's Hill to the deep red gash of the Mareb river, where the thin red track that led to the sea snaked off across the county of Logon and northwards across the stony plain.

"Over there!" cried Abraham, pointing. "Just by the King's Hill! They were stampeding towards those fields there, so I ran upstream, and they followed!"

"They certainly did! That must be where you fell in, and the old she-elephant followed you!"

Lahia squeezed his shoulder, and he squeezed hers. They sat and watched evening begin to fall over their father's town, over the fields and pastures of the county of Logon, and the plains and mountains of his kingdom that stretched out towards the Wild Lands in the west, towards the sea-coast in the north-east, and towards the kingdom of his father's over-lord, the Ras of Tigre, to the south.

"Look!" cried Lahia. "The cows and goats are on their way home. No excitements with elephants this time!" And they sat watching the livestock of Logon and of their own palace, tiny as toys, plodding their way home from all over the surrounding countryside.

Suddenly Abraham stiffened. Up the path from the town came something that flashed in the sun. Spearheads! Shields shining with silver-gilt!

"It's Father!"

They scrambled down from the wall, not caring this time about Abraham's aching joints, and rushed to the hut, where Makeda sat on the door-step in her long white dress, spinning cotton.

"Father is here!"

They left her putting her things away,

and dashed to the gate. The long line of horse-men and load-bearers was reaching the top of the slope, all mixed up with the cows and goats returning from their day's grazing. At the head of the line rode Fares, the Lord of the Sea, on his tall chestnut stallion, Thunder. His cotton shirt, breeches and cloak, that should have been white, were dark with sweat and dried mud, and the tiny braids plaited back along his head were grey with dust. The two children stood by the gate, wondering if they dared come nearer, but suddenly the Lord of the Sea saw them, threw his spears and shield to the horseman next to him and cantered across. Then he reached down and pulled the boy up into his arms.

"Hey! Little monk! So you left your prayers and saved us from a stampede!"

Abraham said nothing, and simply hugged his father back. But then he couldn't help himself, and burst out,

"Oh, Father, WHY weren't you there when I was ill?"

His father's thin, hawk-nosed face look-ed stern.

Abraham Hannibal

"What kind of talk is this? How dare you question the Lord of the Sea!"

For an instant, Abraham thought his father was going to push him down off Thunder's back. But then, suddenly, Fares smiled.

"Well, you're allowed to miss me, I suppose! Anyway, I'm back now, so pull yourself together! There was an important message from the Emperor - a matter of the tax on salt - and the Ras of Tigre wished to discuss it with me. Grown-ups' business; one day you will have to deal with these things too. I have to admit I stayed a little longer: there were lions in the district, and we had a day's hunting. But I think you will be glad of that. Hey! You! Slave! Fetch the special basket! And you! Take the horse!"

Fares, the Lord of the Sea, swung down from his horse and helped Abraham down. By this time, the whole clan were standing by the gate, watching, and Granny Ester, Lahia and Makeda with them. The watchers, from Granny Ester (who was getting very creaky), to the youngest slave-child, bowed to the ground.

But then two slaves came up, struggling with a strange load between them - a kind of basket or cage of sticks, that snarled and bounced. They placed it in front of Abraham and Fares, and the boy squatted down to peer between the sticks. Inside was a lion cub, the colour of a yellow melon, and about twice the size.

"We killed the mother. This little fellow was left, and I had the idea of bringing him back for you. The present of a lion - for a boy with the courage of a lion."

Abraham looked from his father to the basket and back again. He had forgotten his sadness, and was grinning with delight and at the thought that had just struck him,

"Our very own lion, just like the ones in Granny's stories about the Emperor's Palace?" he asked.

Fares, the Lord of the Sea, laughed, and pinched Abraham's chin. "You really are my young monk. So much knowledge!"

But then his face grew harsh, and he turned and shouted out loudly,

"Are all the cattle and goats back yet? Where are their herders? There is an important and private matter to deal with. Herders and servants and slaves! Leave, and go about your duties! I wish my children, my chief warriors and my wives to stay. Gather under the tree. I wish all my sons to stand at my side."

The women and girls sat at his feet, and the sons stood next to him, Abraham, the youngest, at one side of his father, and the crowd of his nineteen half-brothers, right up to Gabre Selassie, Servant of the Trinity, the eldest and really a man by now, jostling for space on the other side. The chief warriors tied up their horses and stood at the back

"You all know what happened last week at the river. Abraham, my youngest son, did an act which will never be forgotten. But what, I ask, of my other sons? What did they do when the enemy came? How did they defend my cattle? How did they defend the crops and the homes of my people? *THEY DID NOT*! If they are not able to drive off a herd of dumb animals, how can I depend on them when the lands of the Lord of the Sea are under threat? They are cowards and lazy good-for-nothings, not worthy to be called my sons! My warriors!

Ethiopia: At Home

Seize them! Tie them up!"

There was absolute stillness. Not a movement, not a sound. People looked at each other in horrified bewilderment. Then the warriors started to collect straps and ropes from their horses, and made their way through the girls and women to tie up the boys, who were standing frozen in disbelief. Mothers and sisters were trying not to sob.

Fares waited till the boys' hands were tied before he went on.

"Tomorrow morning there will be a service of thanksgiving for my son's recovery, in the church, and in the evening there will be a great feast in his honour. But the boys who are no longer my sons will be taken to the top of Mount Damo, where they will stay tied up and under guard, at my pleasure."

Chapter 5

THE LION-CUB

Abraham and Lahia knelt miserably on the floor of their hut, with the lion-cub in his basket between them. The rickety door was closed as firmly as possible, in case he should try to disappear when they let him out. A tiny oil-lamp was the only light.

"How are we expected to enjoy a feast when this is happening to the other boys?" muttered Abraham bitterly. "It doesn't make sense. How can Father *do* such a thing?"

"Shhhh!" Lahia was talking even more quietly than her brother. "Granny Ester says that the Emperors in Gondar often send their sons and nephews to the top of a high mountain to keep them out of mischief. It happened to some of her own brothers.

Maybe Father thinks it's the right thing for a chief to do."

"It's so unfair!" burst out Abraham in fury. "I was just a bit quicker than they were. They'd have done the same if they'd had the chance. And quite a few of them weren't even there - I mean, they weren't even *supposed* to be in charge of the cows."

Lahia grunted. "You mean, the big boys? Well, I know where *they* were. Drinking in a mead-house down in the town. You know how Father always says that a man should never drink till the day's work is done? I knew he was angry with them even before he went to see the Ras of Tigre, because he didn't take them with him. But anyway, what about the lion-cub? It's all very well Father giving him to you, but where are we supposed to keep him? What are we supposed to feed him on?"

"Well, meat, of course," said Abraham.

"Don't be silly. We don't have meat every day. And what about when everyone's fasting? During Lent and Advent there won't be any meat for weeks on end. In any case, he's too little to eat meat."

They peered at the small golden bundle inside the cage. His fierce snarling had faded into sad little whimpers.

"He must be starving," said Abraham, worriedly. "And thirsty. I suppose he needs his mother."

All of a sudden, his present didn't seem such a treat any more.

"How about some warm new milk?" suggested Lahia. "We could maybe beat an egg into it. I'll go and ask Mother if we can have some. You stay with him and cheer him up. Don't let him out till I get back."

At last they were sitting with a calabash of milk and raw egg, ready to let the cub out. Lahia had chosen a long, narrow-necked calabash and made a cone-shaped end for it out of a soft piece of goat-skin, with a hole for the cub to suck at. Very gently, Abraham opened the basket and stroked the soft fur. The cub growled, but only weakly, and let himself be lifted out and held in the boy's arms. Feeding him was a tricky business, especially in the near-darkness. When he felt the calabash pressed against his mouth, he kept turning his head away, but at last Abraham held the cub's jaws open, while Lahia trickled the milk in, for minute after minute, and he began to suck.

The two children looked at each other in delight.

"I think it's going to be all right," whispered Abraham.

"I think so too," whispered Lahia in reply. "What are you going to call him?"

"Well," considered her brother. "One day perhaps he will be a great hunter, like his mother and father before him. I think he should be called Nimrod, after the one in the Bible, because he was a 'mighty hunter before the Lord'."

They practised saying it, "Nimrod! Nimrod!", and stroked him under his chin. But Nimrod the mighty hunter was fast asleep.

Chapter 6

THE FEAST

The next day, after food supplies had been organised, the nineteen boys, their hands still tied, were lined up by a dozen guards to start the four days' journey south to Mount Damo. Their mothers and sisters, Granny Ester, the house-slaves, Makeda, Abraham and Lahia, all gathered to see them go, but they departed in silence. Fares, the Lord of the Sea, was standing with his arms folded, watching, and no one dared say what was in their heart.

In the evening, the feast began, some thirty people in the big downstairs hall of his father's palace. For once, Abraham sat next to his father, among the chief warriors, instead of with the slaves and the children, and his mother sat on his father's other side, the two black faces on either side of Fares' honey-coloured one.

"How would you like to be served before anyone, my young Lord of the Elephants?"

Abraham grinned. "That would be All Wrong, Father." Then he quickly remembered his manners, and said, "But as Your Highness wishes, of course!

"Well, today, it will be All Right. You! Bring us food!"

And the slaves put in front of them the giant sour pancakes, the spiced raw meat and the red-pepper curry with chicken and eggs that he loved so much.

"Start, my boy! Tonight is your night!"

But something was still All Wrong.

"Father, if I am to eat with the grown-ups, could Lahia eat with us too?"

The Lord of the Sea laughed. "Tonight, everything is possible. You! Bring Lahia!"

So a slave fetched Lahia from the far end of the hall, and they feasted together; Abraham even made himself dizzy by drinking a little of the bright yellow honey-mead.

Much later that night, Abraham got up to relieve himself in the yard. He was just going to say hello to Nimrod, who was chained to a post outside his hut, when he suddenly froze. Coming from somewhere was the sound of murmuring voices. There was very little moon, but over by the palace he could just make out two dark figures. He crept round in the shadow of the yard-wall and listened.

"I will have them brought back from

Mount Damo when I think fit. They need to be taught a lesson. The younger boys are harmless enough, but that Gabre Selassie has a look in his eye that I don't like at all. They need to know who is master here."

Then he heard his mother answering,

"My lord, I know that Abraham's distressed. He feels he's the cause of their punishment."

"Our son has to learn that there is no

place for softness in this world. But, I have to say it, he is a fine boy, and a brave boy, in spite of his fondness for books and Bible studies."

"You aren't so ignorant of the Bible yourself. I remember when we were younger ..."

Abraham heard his father laugh softly, and saw him move close to his mother, taking her face in his hands; when he spoke, his voice sounded gentler than he had ever heard it.

"You mean, you remember words like the song of King Solomon? Something like this?"

And, to Abraham's surprise, the Lord of the Sea began to recite words from the Bible, strange and beautiful old words that the boy could only half understand:

"Behold, thou art fair, my love,
Behold, thou art fair; thou hast doves'
eyes.

Thou art black, but lovely
As the tents of Kedar,
As the curtains of Solomon.
Thou art all fair, my love ..."

Ethiopia: At Home

His voice faded, and the two moved closer still.

Abraham, torn between delight and embarrassment, tiptoed back to his hut, completely forgetting to say hello to Nimrod.

Chapter 7

RIVER-GAMES

The next weeks were strange ones for Abraham. The palace compound was very quiet without the other boys. His stepmothers had never been especially friendly, but now they ignored him completely. The younger slaves took over the herding of the cattle. He still went and did it most days, to keep away from the gloomy compound, and Granny Ester would see him off with her usual cry,

"Mind how you go, Abraham, and mind out for kidnappers!"

Abraham didn't actually know anyone personally who had been snatched by slave-raiders when they out herding the animals, or getting water or firewood, but there were lots of stories about it happening.

"I think I'd *rather* be kidnapped than stay around in this hell-hole," he muttered to himself. Even herding the cattle wasn't the same without his brothers. He'd grown up with the slaves, he was good friends with most of them, but that didn't stop him missing his brothers. It would have been all right if Lahia had been allowed out with him, but she mostly had her jobs at home. Every morning when he set out, she would look up from her grain-pounding or sweeping, and wave him goodbye, and he would wonder again why girls weren't allowed to herd cattle.

One glorious day she did slip out, and they went over to the King's Hill, and looked at Where It Had All Happened. They crouched at the top of the steep river-bank and peered down to where the river, swollen by the Big Rains, rushed noisily below. The old she-elephant had long been taken away, for her tusks and her skin.

"I know!" said Lahia excitedly. "Let's climb right down. How are you at swimming?"

"Not very good ... I've tried a few times

when I've been out with the cows. It depends how deep the water is. I don't suppose you've ever tried, have you?"

"Not really. I don't know why, girls never seem to have the chance to swim. But I'd love to try."

And so, clinging with all their fingers and toes onto bushes and tufts of grass and any bits of stone that poked out, they scrambled down the sheer red cliff-side to where the water roared between the rocks, a deep red-brown because of all the soil it had washed away with it. They poked sticks in to test the depth, and at last risked it. In places it didn't even come up to their knees, but they found a few pools where they could lie and splash and feel the water rushing past, trying to tug them downstream, or sit under a little waterfall and feel the flood gushing down over their heads.

That was one of the good days, and they went back to play in the river whenever they could, but most of the time Abraham felt curiously empty and lost. Worse still, his mother was right: he did feel guilty, as if it was his fault that his brothers had been sent away.

Ethiopia: At Home

Nimrod was a big consolation; he was certainly a lot of work. Abraham and Lahia kept on with the milk and egg diet, and looked forward to the next fasting period, when there would be all the milk and eggs Nimrod wanted, since nobody else was allowed to eat any then; unfortunately, they had just missed the two-week fast before the Feast of Our Lady. He stayed chained up overnight, and in the daytime, the two children would take him for walks on his chain. If there were no animals at all around in the yard, they let him loose in there, to the delight of the little girls and the dismay of their mothers.

Chapter 8

CARAVANS

The Big Rains were well and truly over now, the rivers were getting lower, and even from up on Saint Mary's Hill, Abraham could see a buzz down in the town. That long road that snaked north-east from the sea-coast had been empty for months, but now that the highlands were drying out, caravans of donkeys and mules could be seen, making their way inland from the sea; and one day, from up on the hill-top, Abraham even saw the first caravan of the season crawling towards Dibarwa from the south, on its way through to the coast. The market-places and the warehouses were jumping, and not only on Saturday market-day.

Abraham and Lahia loved the

excitement and bustle of the market-places, the babble of different languages the traders spoke, the strange clothes they wore, the smell and the feel of the goods. As soon as they got the chance, they slipped down to see it all close-up once more.

As soon as they came down to the main track that led inland, they bumped into their first caravan making its way up from the coast: some two hundred mules and donkeys, loaded with huge bundles and boxes, picking their way over the sharp rocks and shifting stones of the track. The traders had beards and light brown skins, and wore turbans or head-cloths and full, floor-length robes - Arabs, the children knew that, and even a few from far-away India.

Abraham had been able to spend far more time in the town than Lahia, and he had picked up a good bit of Arabic by now, so he chatted with them cheerfully in their language, with rapid translations for his sister's benefit. The Arabs in charge were riding mules, but not too fast, and the two children were able to jog alongside them.

"Peace be with you!"

"And peace be with you, little brother!"

"What do you have in your loads this time?"

"These here are carpets from Turkey, and rich velvet robes; down the back there's cotton and silk from India. The boxes up ahead are guns from Holland."

The strange foreign names meant nothing to Abraham - he had never seen a map - but he loved the sound of them: there was a magic in them, an excitement ... even a kind of promise ...

"What are those really big boxes?"

"Mirrors, from Venice. Where your sister's beads come from."

"*Mirrors*?" Abraham had only ever seen one mirror, a small one that one of his unfavourite stepmothers had. He couldn't imagine a mirror as big as he was. He fingered Lahia's necklace and explained to her, "That's from Venice."

He turned back to the merchants and asked, "Who is it all for?"

"Some things are for selling to anyone

who will buy, but some are for your Emperor."

"In Gondar? You're going to Gondar?"

"That's right, little brother. Many's the load I've brought to the castles there."

"I'd like to go to Gondar one day."

"If you go much further with us, you'll *be* in Gondar," laughed the merchant.

It was true: they were quite a long way from town already, well ahead of the donkeys, who moved at the pace *they* chose, and well ahead of the donkey-drivers, who moved at the pace the donkeys chose.

"We'll leave you now. Peace be with you all, and a safe journey," called Abraham.

The two children turned round, and walked slowly back to the town, getting their breath back

"The Queen of Sheba must have come with a caravan like that one," said Abraham, thoughtfully. "Except she had camels instead of donkeys - 'camels that bare spices, and very much gold, and precious stones', the Bible says."

"And she was going the other way," pointed out Lahia. "I mean, towards

Jerusalem, not away from it. Even I can work that out, silly!"

But Abraham was day-dreaming about somewhere nearer than Jerusalem.

Gondar! That's the city in Granny Ester's stories, the city where she grew up! Imagine castles full of paintings and precious stones, and forty-four churches full of gold ... Gondar's where the Emperor lives, the Conquering Lion of Judah, the descendant of King Solomon, and he's guarded by real lions, just like Nimrod, only bigger ...

"One day, I'll go there," said Abraham, suddenly.

"Where? Jerusalem?"

"Maybe there too. But I meant Gondar."

"Why not? If you want to do something badly enough and don't give up, you *will* do it in the end."

The most exciting part of Dibarwa was the lower town, where the Muslims lived and traded. Here half-a-dozen little stores had their wares spilling out in front of them, and the children could ruffle the piles of shining rainbow-coloured silks, try out the embroidered slippers and the tasselled umbrellas. Everyone knew whose children they were.

"Peace be with you, children! How goes it up on the hill?" came a cheerful shout. It was Kemal, a young Arab merchant who ran a store selling all kinds of beads and ornaments.

"What's all this I hear about a pet lion up there? You fancy yourself as the Emperor, then, do you, with your own lion roaming round your Palace?"

Abraham grinned, and ran his fingers through the heaps of gleaming, clinking glass beads.

"He wasn't *my* idea. My father gave him to me. But he is the best thing ever. *Very* fierce. You'd be terrified."

Kemal ignored that, and smiled at Lahia.

"We don't see you down here that often, little lady! Choose yourself some beads!"

Lahia turned to Abraham, confused.

"What's he saying, Abraham?"

Abraham explained, and Lahia spent

ages picking out five large clear blue beads with swirling yellow and red patterns inside them; Kemal strung them on a leather string, and put them round her neck, and Abraham taught her how to say thank you in Arabic.

The children moved on. The Muslim merchants sold more every-day goods too, here and in the markets, and the air was full of the smell of coffee and spices, musk and wax and honey, cow-hides and fleecy sheep-skins. There were the grey blocks of salt that were used for money as well as for food, and heaps of grain and dried beans.

Then the children wandered to the upper part of the town, toward the Mareb river, where the Christians lived, and the goldsmiths and silversmiths had their workshops, where a bridegroom could buy a gold necklace for his bride, parents a little silver cross for their baby, or a church a huge silver one for its processions.

The children made their way to one particular workshop. Sitting working on a pair of gold ear-rings was a small round white man.

"Greetings, Yanni!" called the children.

Abraham Hannibal

Yanni the Greek jumped. "Don't *do* that, children, when I'm deep in work. It's not good for my heart. Will you have some lemonade?"

Soon they were all sitting on Yanni's rich bright carpets (he always refused to call them Turkish carpets) in his living-room, drinking freshly-squeezed lemon juice with sugar - something they never had anywhere else. Yanni had lived here nearly all his life and spoke the language well. Abraham had seen three or four other white men in his time, but Yanni was the only one he really knew.

"I can tell you children, your father's country is a fine one, for a Christian. Where I come from, the Turks never give us a moment's peace. New taxes every day, new rules and regulations about what you can and can't wear, churches all turned into mosques. It was the day a Turkish soldier insulted my sister that I had to leave. I didn't have a weapon at the time, or I'd have had a man's blood on my conscience forever, but I punched him in the face so hard half his teeth fell out. I escaped in a little fishing boat, got all the way to Africa, to Alexandria. Of course, I was younger and fitter then."

Ethiopia: At Home

Abraham tried to avoid meeting Lahia's eye. Every time he met Yanni he'd been told a different version of this story, and by now he didn't believe any of them. When Lahia couldn't come to town with him, he used to report back to her the version he'd just been told, and they would take turns acting Yanni telling the story until they collapsed into giggles. But he was a kind old man, and friendly, and they never teased him to his face.

At last, they couldn't put off going home any longer. As they crossed the town, a caravan came plodding through from up-country, ready to rest for the night. The children could see the great tusks of ivory, strapped one on each side of the weary donkeys, the sacks of grain and skins of butter and honey, the locked chests of gold, all on their way to the sea-coast and a hundred different destinations.

In silence, peeking round the corner of a warehouse, Abraham and Lahia watched another part of the caravan that was not on donkey-back, but was making its own way to the sea-coast. About four dozen children, a dozen young women, and a few men, their hands chained in front of them, filed into the market place, and slumped down on the ground to rest. By the look of them, their clothes and their hair and their faces, they came from all kinds of different lands. The merchants - some Arabs and some local men - stood guard with guns, but the slaves didn't look inclined to escape: they just looked bewildered, miserable, and very tired.

"From the Wild Lands, mostly, I think," whispered Lahia. "Maybe some of them speak our secret language."

In the language of the Kunama, the children whispered greetings to the slaves, and some of the limp figures raised their heads in curiosity. But it was no use. One of the guards heard them too, and was next to them in a few quick strides, beating them away with the barrel of his musket, and screaming,

"Scat! Get lost, kids! Unless you'd like to join your brothers and sisters on the trip?"

The children fled, and didn't stop till they were halfway up Saint Mary's Hill.

"That really was scary," panted Lahia. "I think he meant it, don't you?"

Ethiopia: At Home

"I think so," gasped Abraham in reply. "But the other Arabs, earlier on, were so friendly. And so are the Arabs in town."

"Well, we have been warned before," said Lahia. "As Granny Ester says, 'Mind how you go, and mind out for kidnappers.' Just because someone's a Christian, or even the child of a chief, doesn't mean they can't be kidnapped. *Anyone* can end up a slave."

It was a relief to get back even to the depressing atmosphere of the royal compound. And later that night, after Abraham and his sister had settled themselves for sleep on their cow-skins on the hut floor, he heard her softly call him,

"Abraham!"

"Yes?"

"Have you ever thought that if ... if Father hadn't loved Mother so much, she'd have been sold, just like those Slave-People today? She could've been marched off to the sea in a caravan just like that!"

"And so would we!"

"There wouldn't have *been* any us, silly! We would never have been born!"

Abraham thought about it for a moment. It was a disturbing idea.

"I'm *glad* you were born, Lahia. I like having you for a sister."

Lahia laughed.

"Yes, you *are* lucky, aren't you! But then, I think *I'm* lucky too."

Chapter 9

JOURNEY TO THE EMPEROR

Then the bustle of the town seemed to spread even to the palace on the hill. Servants were up and down to the markets and warehouses five times a day, the Lord of the Sea was around more than usual, and strode around giving orders for packing and loading, and a new corral was built outside the yard-wall. Young horses were brought in from the countryside every evening, and stabled in the corral every night; every night, there were more of them. One evening, Fares called Abraham to his palace. The Lord of the Sea sat cross-legged on his throne; the boy squatted at his feet.

"So, little monk! Let's see what you know

of the business of ruling! What do you make of all the preparations here these days?" asked Fares.

Abraham frowned. "Are you taking presents to the Emperor in Gondar, like last year, Father?"

Fares smiled. "In a way. It's the time of the yearly tribute. Each year, the great lords of the empire have to pay part of our wealth to

the Emperor, and I am one of the wealthiest. Do you know why?"

Abraham shook his head.

"Every grain of food, every ounce of ivory or gold, that leaves Ethiopia by sea, has to go through my domain, on its way to the seaport of Massawa. So does every luxury foreign article, every gun, every bead and bottle, that is brought into the empire through the port. The merchants pay me a tax on all the goods going in or out. Apart from the taxes the farmers pay me on their crops, this is the chief source of my wealth, and every year, the Emperor takes his share of that. Here, our tribute is mostly horses, guns, and rich cloth. I leave in two days' time for Gondar, to present my tribute."

A thought that had long puzzled Abraham came back to him. "Father, may I ask you a question? Does Massawa belong to you?"

"Why do you ask?"

"Well, you're called the Lord of the Sea, and so I think the sea and the coast and the ports ought to belong to you."

"I think the Emperor and I would agree

with you, little monk! Well, once upon a time they *did* belong to the Lord of the Sea and his Emperor, but the Turks came in their ships from far away. They had guns, and we did not, and they took the sea-coast away from us, so that now it belongs to their Sultan. The name of the Lords of the Sea never changed, because one day, perhaps, we shall be Lords of the Sea again. But enough of the old days! How would you like to come to Gondar with me?"

Abraham's eyes and mouth grew wide.

"More than anything else in the world, Father!"

"It's settled, then."

Of course, there was the dark side. There was no question of Lahia being allowed to go, and Abraham had to say goodbye to his mother too, and Granny Ester - and to Nimrod. He and Lahia sat in a shady corner of the hot courtyard, where Nimrod lay dozing at the end of his chain, each of them rubbing one of his big soft ears.

Ethiopia: At Home

"You will look after him, won't you, Lahia?"

"He will be grown-up, fat and happy when you come back - and *very* fierce."

"Not towards me. Never. He'll remember me."

The day Abraham set off, before first light, Lahia and Makeda didn't come down to the town to see him off. They hugged each other good-bye without a word inside the dark hut, so that no one would see their tears. Then his sister and mother made their way to the yard-wall where it towered high above the track that led inland. They climbed up and sat with their arms around each other, watching the long caravan toiling south, until the last donkey was out of sight and the sun blazed fiercely through the thin air of High Ethiopia.

Chapter 10

AFRICAN ZION

Forty-one days, the journey took. Abraham kept count. Every night when he curled up inside his cloak to sleep, whether in a village hut, or in the compound of a rich local lord, or in a rough shelter of branches against the mountain cold, or most often, simply under the stars, he cut a mark in his stick. He had his own white mule, Butterfly, who had a sweet face and a loving nature, but got her name because she had a mind that flitted madly from one thing to another. At first it was fun riding her, being up so high, but he soon took to walking most of the time, while she went ahead, so that he could chat to the donkey drivers. His father was riding his favour-

Ethiopia: The Journey

ite stallion, Thunder. Abraham had ridden Thunder. Once. It had been two whole dry seasons ago …three of his half-brothers had dared him to, and he'd done it. They'd been herding the cattle one hot noon-tide, and they'd found the slave who was looking after their father's horses fast asleep. Abraham cut the rope hobbling Thunder's front legs himself, and his brothers had lifted him up – he could never have mounted that great shining ebony cliff by himself. He had been too small to grip Thunder's flanks with his knees, so he had twisted his hands into the stallion's mane, wrapped his legs round his neck, and then whispered into his ear, "GO, Thunder, GO! Go like the wind!"

And Thunder had gone, galloping madly, bucking and leaping through the thorn-scrub, over the dry stream-beds, round the great stands of umbrella-cactus, further and further towards the Wild Lands, until at last he had stumbled over a stone and pitched the boy onto the hard dry earth.

It was growing dark by the time Abraham limped home; Thunder had made *his* way back hours before. Fares beat him, of course, but not nearly as hard as he might have done, and Abraham thought he could see a glint of pride in his father's eyes as he shouted at him, "What business has a boy of your age riding his lord's horses?" Besides – it had been worth it for the swoosh of the wind on his skin, and the rushing of the stony ground below Thunder's hooves ...

But Abraham was two whole years older now, and he was leaving his home and his brothers behind. There were steep and chilly mountains to cross soon after leaving home, then the Mareb river. It was far wider than he knew it at home, but not too deep, and even silly Butterfly and the loaded donkeys waded across without too much trouble. Then there was a long, long plain, where mountains sharp as knife-blades, thin as sheets of parchment, jabbed up sheer into the sky, and filled his dreams at night.

Then they arrived in the town of Aksum, which looked quite ordinary at first sight - a bit like Dibarwa, but not as big or as busy - but where Abraham's beloved *Stories of the Kings* came alive. First of all, they went to pray in a church quite different from every church Abraham had ever seen, for the churches he knew were all round, and this one was long, with four corners!

"You are doing an act that God will remember on Judgement Day, Abraham, by praying in the church of Our Lady of Zion," said Fares, the Lord of the Sea, as they kissed the door-posts of the church, and went to stand in front of the Holy of Holies.

"Why is that?"

"Because the Tablets of the Law that Moses brought down from Mount Sinai, and the Ark of the Covenant that he built to hold them, are here in this church. There, right in front of us."

Abraham looked at the Holy of Holies, its wooden doors closed tight, and its outside walls covered with paintings, like bigger versions of the pictures in Abba Mikail's *Stories of the Kings*, and tried to imagine what was inside.

"Do you remember the story, little monk?"

"You mean, how the Emperor Menelik took the holy Ark of the Covenant from the

temple of his father Solomon in Jerusalem, and brought it to his mother's land?"

"Good boy! This *is* the land of Sheba, here around Aksum - this is Queen Makeda's country. Outside are the great stones that the grandsons of Menelik built."

So when they had prayed, they went out to marvel at the gigantic solid stone obelisks that were old when Jesus was born - so people said. One of them had long since fallen and smashed, but another towered over the huge old sycamore tree behind, taller by far than any building Abraham had ever seen.

Chapter 11

THE TERRIBLE RIVER

But, for all the marvels of Aksum and the Queen of Sheba's country, it was the days ahead that really burnt themselves into Abraham's memory.

Like Day 19, the day they crossed the Terrible River.

Its valley was terrible enough: a long, slow, tricky climb down, the magnificent tribute horses and the loaded donkeys and mules behind and in front of them slipping and stumbling in the loose dry soil, and the air getting hotter and heavier with every step down, although the sun was not yet up. The Big Rains were over long ago, but the river was full, fast-moving, and very wide.

As they got nearer the bottom of the valley, Abraham riding Butterfly, and Fares, the Lord of the Sea, on Thunder, they could see the wide sandy beach below them full of warriors and donkey-drivers, rushing towards the water, screaming at the tops of their lungs, hurling stones and bits of branch, anything that came to hand, into the water, firing their muskets. Abraham looked wildly from this scene of madness to his father's face, and in spite of himself reached over, as if to take hold of his arm. His father laughed.

"Don't worry. They're just chasing away the crocodiles. We've no time to lose. We need to start crossing at once. I don't want anyone spending the night down here. There's disease in these hot valleys."

They watched while the men let the horses drink, and then started leading them into the water. The valley echoed with sound of neighing, shouting and cursing, and then the first horses started swimming across, their

riders hanging on to their tails. A cheer went up from Abraham's side when the first horse and rider came up, dripping, on the other bank.

Abraham went to give Butterfly and himself a drink, keeping a careful look out for crocodiles, and then tied her up in the shade of a tree.

"She'll need all the rest she can get if she's going to swim across *that*," he muttered to

himself. He didn't like to think what he might
need to make the same journey.

Meanwhile, the donkey and mule drivers
were starting to unload their pack-animals.

"How are the loads going to get across,
Father?"

"You'll see. Look!"

Behind them on the bank, the donkey-
drivers and a crowd of men and women from
the last village were gathered round, and were

doing mysterious things with ropes and sticks and animal skins.

Abraham went across to investigate.

"Rafts! Are you making rafts?"

The villagers nodded. The ground was piled with blown-up goatskins, like heaps of headless bodies. He picked one up, and it was light as a handful of cotton. They were tying them underneath rough wooden platforms.

Abraham looked from the rafts to the enormous stacks of goods that needed to get across and exclaimed,

"Are we ever going to do it?"

He thought of the bright silks and velvets inside the bundles: they would never survive a wetting. And although he didn't know much about guns, he knew they didn't like water either.

About half the donkeys and mules were across by now, and the Lord of the Sea announced,

"Right! Let's get us two across now. Not nervous, are you, little monk? I'll be right next to you."

Abraham grinned brightly, and set about

strapping his few belongings onto Butterfly's back.

It all started off fine. Butterfly waded in with only a bit of head-tossing and eye-rolling, and then he followed. The water felt very warm; soon it was up to his chest and he knew that he'd have to let his feet come up from the bottom. He twisted Butterfly's tail firmly round one hand and started swimming. He could feel Butterfly thrusting strongly through the water, pulling him across. The current was strong, but the mule was stronger. To his left (the upstream side) he could just see, out of the corner of his eye, his father and Thunder doing the same.

"Hey, little monk? Enjoying your swim?"

He was concentrating too hard to answer, but as a matter of fact, it was *almost* beginning to be fun. And everything carried on fine until about the middle of the river. Then, he never knew how, everything turned hideous.

There were donkeys and mules swimming across on his right (the downstream side), as well as in front of him. Maybe

Abraham Hannibal

Butterfly got kicked by the donkey in front of her, or some water went up her nose, or maybe it was just that the current got too strong, but suddenly she started panicking, whinnying and choking as she breathed in water, plunging and rolling and splashing. He held on to her tail for dear life as he was pulled this way and that, his head tugged under the water and out again; he choked as he breathed in a great gasp of water.

Suddenly he felt a hand under his armpit, and knew that his father was holding him; he let go Butterfly's tail. But Butterfly must have kicked the donkey on her right, because it started panicking too, bucking and snorting and spluttering.

By the time Thunder had pulled him and his father across, and they were standing panting and dripping on the bank, watching the river, Butterfly had calmed down, and was swimming quietly across as though nothing had happened. But the donkey that Butterfly had kicked was being swept downstream in an awful hubbub of splashing and choking - every watcher stood silently, following it with his eyes

Ethiopia: The Journey

- until, just before the distant bend in the river, a long scaly shape slid off a rock and swam towards the beast. There was a sudden stillness, and the donkey vanished under the water.

Chapter 12

THE END OF BUTTERFLY

The rest of the journey to Gondar seemed one long "up". Up out of the hot river valley, then up and up and up, along a dreadful path, all loose stones or slippery rock, with a sheer cliff above and a sheer cliff below, hardly wide enough for a boy, never mind a loaded donkey. Even with his tough-soled bare feet and their strong toes, used to scrambling and clinging onto rocks, Abraham had some nasty scares. Often the path disappeared altogether. And when it did go down, that only meant that it soon went up again even further, to make up for it.

The air soon became cooler, and at night it was miserably cold. The houses they passed seemed flimsy things for such a cold place, not sturdy stone with solid roofs like the houses at home, but round huts of sticks and clay with straw roofs. The villagers seemed friendly enough, though they spoke quite a different language from his. He knew it was the language of Gondar, because Granny Ester often used to talk in it, especially when she told her stories of the marvels of the palace where she had grown up, and Father used to speak it with some of their most important visitors.

Poor Butterfly. Maybe she had panicked stupidly in the Terrible River, but she still didn't deserve what happened on Day 32. Abraham was walking, not riding, not because he was chatting to anyone (there wasn't room to walk side-by-side, and besides, he didn't have any spare breath), but because he felt safer on his own two feet. And, as it turned out, that was a wise decision. It was getting dark, darker than they normally travelled in this difficult countryside, but the only place open enough for a camp was still some way ahead.

Suddenly, above the noise of gentle pant-

ing, the occasional whinny, the *clop-clop*! and scuffle of hooves on the rocks, there was a loud, rushing *BOOM*! and a mass of rocks was suddenly roaring down the mountainside above the path.

It hit the path just in front of Butterfly, carrying away the two mules ahead of her, and tearing a great gap before it carried on down the slope. Butterfly, terrified by the noise and the speed of all this, and faced with a big hole in front of her, reared up on her hind-legs, came down awkwardly, stumbled, and knocked the edge of the path away. And Abraham was able to see, from the far side of the hole, through the grey twilight, the white form of Butterfly slither over the edge, and with a last neigh of despair, hurtle down into the darkness.

Chapter 13

THE EMPEROR'S PALACE

The sun was at its highest, and he had to squeeze up his eyes against the fierce glare, when he first saw Gondar. The steep path was levelling out, and the caravan was beginning to spread over the hillside, when there, up above him, was the city: a great mass of straw-thatched huts with green trees in between, and above them, like the pictures of Jerusalem in *Stories of the Kings*, the high stone walls of the palace compound, and behind the walls, the towers and battlements of the royal castles.

GONDAR!

"Abraham!" called Fares, the Lord of the Sea.

"Yes, Father."

"You will ride with me through the city. Mount your mule."

They had found a replacement mule for Abraham, a steady brown mare called Trusty, but he normally only rode her when he was desperately tired. He and his father and some dozen of his chief warriors left the caravan on the outskirts of the city, and rode through the dusty alleyways until they came to the high brown battlemented walls, and their herald blew his horn in front of a huge gate.

They were led through a great courtyard full of stone buildings, not just two-storeyed like his father's palace, but looming three and four storeys high, with towers higher still, and with more windows, and bigger ones, than he had ever seen in his life, past a big square fish-pond, and through the great door of one of the palaces; then through room after room, their walls and ceilings glowing with paintings and gold, until at last they were led into a hall where at the far end sat cross-legged on his throne the King of Kings, the Conquering Lion of the Tribe of Judah, the Emperor Jesus the Great, surrounded by rows of his great

lords, all standing in absolute silence.

Abraham watched to see what his father was going to do. Fares, the Lord of the Sea, strode forward to the throne and lay down flat on the floor, then knelt and kissed the Emperor's foot, three times in all.

"The Lord of the Sea has brought the King of Kings the tribute that is his due," rang out his father's voice.

The Emperor nodded.

"The King of Kings thanks the Lord of the Sea for his gifts. His followers may approach."

One by one, Abraham, and then the chiefs, did as his father had done. Then there were endless grand speeches on both sides, but Abraham wasn't listening, he was looking.

It was wonderful - like standing in the middle of a picture in *Stories of the Kings*. The whole room, even the ceiling, was painted with palm-trees, except where it had huge mirrors set into the walls, in ivory frames. (To think that every one of those mirrors had crossed the Terrible River!)

The throne was of gold, with red and

gold cushions, and Jesus the Great himself was a blaze of colour and gold in a long robe of blue velvet with huge dangling sleeves, and little gold flowers all over it. He had a gold-striped veil round his head and pulled across his mouth, and curly-toed slippers with pearls all over them. Abraham stared and stared at him.

I wouldn't want to get on the wrong side of HIM! He does have sensible eyes, but they've got a strict sort of look about them, like Father on one of his angry days ...

The lords were all wearing the most amazing bright robes - he didn't even know the names of the colours - with gold bracelets and brooches galore. And then suddenly, Abraham jumped: at the end of the front row stood a white man - but not like Yanni at all. He was much paler, for a start, with curiously light eyes, a sort of sky-blue, and he didn't have a beard. And although he didn't seem very old, his hair was like a huge white sheep's fleece, or maybe a thorn-tree in blossom. He wore strange tight leg-coverings, right down to his big shiny shoes with heavy high heels, and a funny wide-skirted coat, decorated with silver. He caught Abraham staring and, very slowly, winked one of his sky-blue eyes. Abraham, embarrassed, looked down at his feet.

Suddenly, as Abraham was in a daydream about Nimrod and where the Emperor kept *his* lions, he heard his name.

"He is a young boy to make such a long journey, my lord, but it was a kind of reward. Grandmothers by the fireside are already telling stories about his deeds."

"Is that so, Fares? Tell us all, if you and he are not too tired."

And the Lord of the Sea told the story of the elephants, with Abraham's narrow escapes in the Terrible River and on the mountainside thrown in for good measure. Everyone clapped politely at the end, and Abraham could see the white man staring at him while someone whispered busily into his ear - translating, he supposed, into the white man's language.

"So, Abraham!" said the Emperor. "It seems as if you have great things ahead of you, if you have started so young. Come here!"

Abraham stepped right up onto the base

of the throne, and the King of Kings put his hands on his shoulders and looked at him.

"You will make a good friend for my son Allem. You and he are of an age."

Chapter 14

DOCTOR PONCET

So Abraham was taken to play with Prince Allem. There were two questions he had to ask him straight away.

"Where does your father keep the lions?"

"Oh, they're wandering around somewhere. I'll take you to their house."

So they looked at the House of the Lions, and watched the two huge lions wandering in and out of all the palaces as they pleased, and went and talked to them and rubbed their ears. They went to look at the House of the Pigeons as well, where Abraham remembered his other question.

"Who is that white man in your father's court?"

Prince Allem laughed. "Oh, that's our

doctor. Doctor Poncet. He's a Frank, from a place called France, but he lives in Egypt. He's a good doctor. Father and all of us were sick, so a messenger brought him from Cairo to make us well, and now we're all fine again. He'll be going back to Egypt soon."

For a month, Abraham had nothing to do but play. The first two weeks were blissful. There was the King's Bath just outside the city, with a two-storey palace right in the middle of a big shallow pool that was filled by a fast, clear stream. He and Allem went a few times and splashed and ducked each other and played at throwing and catching sticks across the water. Abraham began to wish that he hadn't been ordered to play with Allem: the young Prince had a bad habit of whining if Abraham got a bit rough, though he was even rougher himself.

One day, however, they made a most interesting discovery. They were making their way to the King's Bath, earlier than usual in the morning, when they realised that Doctor Poncet was ahead of them, going the same way. He was carrying a big bag, and wearing a great flowing Arab robe instead of his normal clothes, with his head tied up in a big cloth, like an Indian trader. The two boys stopped and grabbed hold of each other.

"Do you think he's going to have a swim too?" whispered Abraham.

Allem nodded, grinning. "Maybe we should go away." But he didn't sound very convinced.

"D'you know something that's been bothering me?" carried on Abraham. "Are white people like Doctor Poncet white all over, or is it just the bits that show that are white?"

"Well, now's our chance to find out," whispered Allem.

The two boys crept through the trees after the comical figure in its turban and baggy robe. The doctor was still wearing his stiff high-heeled shoes, and every now and then he would trip on the rough ground and mutter what sounded like curses in some foreign language. At last he got to the pool, which had a stream running into it and out of the other side, and went round to where the water flowed out of it. He opened his bag, took out an assortment of little bottles and boxes and a mirror, and put them carefully at the edge of the pool. Then he took off his turban. Underneath was no fleecy white bush, but just a pale scalp with very, very short straw-coloured hair. The boys, peeking from behind a bush, stared at each other.

"I knew that his white hair wasn't real," whispered Allem. "He's taken it off and shown me his head before now."

Now the doctor was kicking off his shoes, stripping off his stockings. At last the moment came, and he picked up the skirts of his robe and pulled it up over his head and off. He was naked, and white from head to foot, as white as a peeled egg. If anything, his head and hands and neck were the darkest bits, reddened and leathery from the sun. The two boys clamped their hands over their mouths to stifle their giggles, and rolled around silently on the ground behind their bush.

There was a big splash. Doctor Poncet was in! The boys peered round again, and watched the longest and most complicated performance of creaming, foaming, rinsing,

gargling, singing, splashing, rubbing and ducking. Then the doctor scraped at his cheeks with a kind of knife, standing in the water with the mirror in front of him on the edge of the pool. The boys had never seen a man shave before, and gazed in astonishment. At last he got out and dried himself with a cloth, and started creaming himself with something else, singing all the while.

"He's going to be finished soon," whispered Abraham. "What a shame!"

He hunted around him, and found what he was looking for: a nice smooth round pebble. While Allem looked on, puzzled, Abraham stood up and took careful aim at Doctor Poncet's shiny white backside. The pebble whizzed through the air and ... PHUT! dented the soft flesh of its target.

Doctor Poncet's song changed into a howl as his hand flew to his bruised backside. He started running, naked and barefoot as he was, towards the boys' hiding-place, but Abraham and Allem didn't stay around. The doctor hobbled after them for a little while as they darted back towards Gondar, but soon gave up, and went back, muttering, to get on with his dressing.

The boys stopped for a minute when they were safely out of sight and ear-shot.

"What d'you do that for?" panted Allem. "I bet he recognised us. If you get me into trouble with my father, I'm going to tell them it was your fault, you idiot!"

"Don't you call me an idiot," snapped Abraham furiously. "You're just chicken! AND you're a sneak!" And he grabbed Prince Allem round the neck and wrestled him to the ground, thumping him hard in the chest.

Allem gave as good as he got, but not for long. Soon he wriggled out from Abraham's grip, and ran off home to the palace, whimpering.

The days went by. There was plenty for Abraham to do in the royal compound, plenty to explore, right up to the roofs of the castles, to what they called "balconies", where Abraham made himself feel sick by looking down such a distance to the ground. The boys heard no more of the incident at the King's Bath; nor did they mention it to each other.

One evening, Abraham climbed up to one of the balconies, and got a terrible shock. There was Doctor Poncet sitting, in his normal fancy clothes and big white hair, looking at the sun sinking down towards the mountain-tops. Abraham thought of sneaking down the stairs again, but it was too late: the white man had seen him.

"Greetings, Abraham," said Poncet in the language of Gondar, but that seemed to be all he could say. They stared at each other in silence. Abraham couldn't get out of his mind the picture of the naked doctor chasing after him and Allem, roaring in fury. Certainly he didn't look angry now; in fact, he looked quite amused. Abraham had a bright idea, and asked,

"Do you speak Arabic?"

The doctor did indeed speak Arabic, and they were soon chatting,

"Allem says you are going back to Cairo soon," said Abraham. "Will you be going by camel?"

Ethiopia: Gondar

"I am going further than Cairo, my boy, and not by camel - except for one small part of the journey. I am going all the way to my country, to France, to take letters from your king to mine."

"Tell me about your country. What is the king's name?"

"He is called the Sun King, because his power and his glory shine more brightly than the sun itself. He is the most magnificent ruler in all the world."

Abraham began to wonder if *all* white people were windbags, like his old friend Yanni the Greek and this doctor ....

"But his true name is Louis, the fourteenth of that name," went on the Frank.

"Is his palace as fine as this?"

"Oh, they cannot be compared. This palace compound could fit ... maybe ... twenty times ... into the chief palace of the Sun King. I can show you pictures, when it is light again tomorrow."

And the doctor told Abraham tales of the Sun King's palace, with a hall of a hundred mirrors each as tall as a tree, of banquets lit by ten thousand candles, of gardens where stone images of men and animals spouted water high into the air, and trees were clipped into fantastical shapes, of wheeled carriages which you could climb inside, pulled by horses that galloped as fast as the wind, of fine ladies with dresses as wide as the whole balcony, and hair piled an arm's length high ...

The doctor even took his hair off again, and showed Abraham his bare head, and told him how in the land of the Franks, all people of good birth, men and women, wore false hair, except for sleeping ...

He went on till darkness fell, and they had an awkward time climbing down, but the very next morning, the doctor kept his promise. They met under a shady tree near the House of the Lions, and the doctor was holding a fat little book in his hands.

"This book tells of some of the great things in my country. Look here, at the first picture. This is the Sun King."

There he was, in his big bushy wig, and clothes like Doctor Poncet's on a special occasion, standing in a huge fancy room, with

Sa Majesté Louis XIV

a crown on a table next to him. His face was much harder than the doctor's ... not a friendly face at all. The drawing was quite different from what Abraham was used to: somehow it looked much more ... well ... *real* ... than the pictures on church walls or in *Stories of the Kings*. And yet there were no colours in it at all; it was done just with black lines.

"Why didn't the monk paint it with colours?" asked Abraham.

Poncet smiled. "Oh, in France monks stopped painting pictures in books and copying the words long, long ago. Somebody *did* draw this picture, but not in the way you mean. He just drew the picture once, and then something called a ... a ... machine, a printing press ... made thousands of copies, all exactly the same. It did all the words, too. These machines are very clever, and very fast. They just can't do colours. Not yet, anyway."

Abraham gaped in amazement. "Explain it all over again, please. Everything, this time."

So Doctor Poncet did, and then they looked at the book. There they were, the fountains, the statues, the mirrors, the carriages, the fine ladies and gentlemen, just as the Doctor had described them. Every chapter ended with a little sign, like a flower with three pointed petals.

"What's that thing?" asked Abraham.

"Oh, that's the lily-flower, the sign of France, like the lion that your Emperor uses as a sign of Ethiopia. Look, here it is again!"

Soon Abraham was spotting them all over the pictures in the book, but he soon got tired of that.

"Tell me some more stories about the land of the Franks, and more stories about machines, Doctor Poncet!"

So there were more tales about the wonders of France, and many more on other days too, and every now and then, Abraham felt guilty about throwing that pebble at his new friend's backside. Neither of them ever mentioned the King's Bath, and he never *could* be sure whether the doctor knew it had been him, or not ... but sometimes he saw a twinkly sort of look in his eyes, and he wondered ...

But there were other things to do in Gondar too. Almost better than the King's

Abraham Hannibal

Bath was the new church that the Emperor was having built on one of the hills near the town, and Abraham could go and watch the painters as they worked, covering every inch of the walls with picture-stories. They soon started letting Abraham help mix the paint and get the brushes ready, and even have a go at painting. Soon he was spending part of every day there.

The only thing that came near to spoiling the holiday was Prince Allem. There was a chill between the boys now, ever since their fight, and anyway, he was a grumpy kind of boy, always complaining about everything and everybody. So whenever he could, Abraham spent his time with Doctor Poncet and the older boys or even the princesses.

But in any case, everything was about to change for ever.

Chapter 15

SENTENCED TO EXILE

It was the last banquet before the big Lent fast began, and their farewell banquet too; soon the Small Rains would begin, the country would disappear under mud and flood, and the journey back home would become impossible. Abraham was sitting at the far end of the hall, sharing a dish and chattering with the other children, when a slave came to call them all up to the Emperor's table.

Jesus the Great, his Empress, all the great lords and their wives, and Fares, the Lord of the Sea, and all of *his* lords were sitting there, looking very full and a bit drunk. The slaves were clearing up around them, and bringing water for them to wash their hands. And, to

Abraham's surprise, Doctor Poncet was there too.

"Children!" bellowed the Emperor over the noise in the hall. "We have been speaking of the departure of our good Frankish friend, Doctor Poncet. Soon you, my friends from Dibarwa, will leave on your journey north, and not long afterwards, this noble foreigner who has done me and my family such service, must return to his home. He will be taking a letter from me to my brother, the King of France. He will also be taking splendid gifts. We have decided on gold, an elephant, and some of our finest horses. But we would like also to send some of our noble young children to his court, to learn the ways of France, and show the Franks that the youth of Ethiopia is second to none for wisdom, courage, and high breeding."

He paused, and looked up and down the group of listening girls and boys.

"The royal line of Solomon should be represented, I feel ... Allem, I have a mind to send *you* to France, the finest country in the world."

Ethiopia: Gondar

Abraham saw Allem swallow hard. He opened his mouth, shut it again and then said, in a funny kind of croak:

"My royal father, if it is your pleasure that I should make that voyage, then I will undertake it with joy, but it would be a great sorrow for me to be separated from you."

And he bowed down flat on the ground.

"He's cleverer than I thought," said Abraham to himself. "Little toad!"

Jesus the Great turned to the translator, and said, "Ask the doctor how they would treat my son at the court of the Sun King."

The answer came back, "He would be treated with all the honours due to the greatest and most powerful king in Africa."

The Emperor sat and thought for a little while. "He's too young," he suddenly announced. "The voyage is too long and difficult. Maybe later, when he has more years over his head."

The older children of the Emperor started eying each other nervously. Jesus the Great, the Lion of Judah, looked them up and down again. Then his eyes fixed on Abraham.

"You, my boy! You are young, but you are already a hardened traveller. You have shown your courage time and time again, and you are of the line of Solomon. You shall go to France. Fares, do you hear me? Your son shall go to France. He shall show the King of the Franks what the youth of Ethiopia are made of, and how they are worthy children of Solomon."

Abraham did not sleep that night. The room was horribly hot, and the other children never seemed to stop coughing and snoring and fidgeting.

Imagine never seeing home again, or Mother, or Lahia, or Nimrod ... My brothers are still up on Mount Damo - maybe I won't even be able to say goodbye to them ... Imagine never going hunting with Father ... No more swimming in the Mareb river, no more Granny Ester and her stories, no more Abba Mikail and drawing Bible pictures ... Imagine leaving them all behind for ever ... well, almost certainly for ever ...

And he remembered the warning expression on his father's face when he had wanted to protest to the Emperor and beg him not to send him away; he thought of the words his father muttered at him as they all left the hall,

"Don't even think about refusing. It's no use. He's the Emperor."

And then Abraham thought, again, *That little creeping toad, Allem!*

Chapter 16

HOME AGAIN

The next months passed in a kind of mad nightmare. It turned out that Doctor Poncet, who had come to Ethiopia from Egypt along the Nile, was going back the other way, up the Red Sea from the sea-port of Massawa. On his way north to Massawa, he would be passing right through Abraham's home in Dibarwa, but he wasn't ready to go yet: the horses and the elephant and the other noble children still hadn't been arranged, and a man called Murad, who was going to be the Emperor's special messenger to King Louis, wasn't ready either.

Abraham and his father had the same idea: they begged the Emperor that Abraham should go ahead with his father and wait for

Ethiopia: At Home

Poncet in Dibarwa, since that way he would be able to spend longer at home before the final farewell.

And so Fares the Lord of the Sea, his son, his warriors, his mules, his donkeys and his donkey-drivers, all made their way back down the mountains, across the Terrible River, through the Queen of Sheba's country with its church of Our Lady of Zion and the mysterious obelisks, and across the long plain with the nightmare peaks, and so back home to Dibarwa.

Abraham's brothers were brought back from their mountain-top, their punishment over, and life continued, on the surface, quite as normal. But Abraham and Lahia had a secret. As soon as he told her the news, she said, quietly but very firmly,

"I'm coming with you. I'll ask the Frankish doctor as soon as he arrives."

"But what about mother - and father? How can you leave them?"

"I've got a choice, and I've made it. You know what I feel - if you want to do something badly enough, and don't give up, you'll do it in the end."

Nimrod knew their secret too. He *had* recognised Abraham, of course, even after eight months or so, and it was quite a shock when this powerful young beast leapt up to greet him by licking his face. He wasn't nearly full-grown yet, but he certainly wasn't just a cuddly little bundle of golden fur any more. The evening after Lahia told Abraham of her decision, he sat down in the half-dark of the courtyard next to Nimrod, put his arm round his shoulders, and rubbed him under his chin, the way he loved.

"We're going to leave you, Nimrod," he whispered. "Lahia and I are going to leave you. We have to go to a cold land far away, and we can't take you with us. Don't think badly of us, Nimrod. We won't forget you, *ever*. You're the best lion in the world. Mother will look after you. I promise."

And Nimrod nuzzled Abraham's chin, and growled back at him, but gently.

If Lahia's secret plan was some consolation, the attitude of his two least favourite stepmothers drove him wild, but, as usual, there was no-one he dared tell except Lahia and Nimrod. Whenever they had the chance, it was,

"You must feel *honoured* to be selected for such an important mission, Abraham."

or

"Are you feeling excited yet? The Frankish doctor will be here soon."

In fact Doctor Poncet didn't arrive till the middle of July with the nine other children, five girls and four boys, after an especially tricky journey through the Rains. The poor young elephant had died on the way, and Murad, the Emperor's special messenger, was still coming with the horses. Lahia lost no time.

"Let's go and ask the doctor. Now."

Poncet beamed cheerfully as Abraham explained their request to him.

"Why not? One girl more in our group of ten - why not? It's better that you should have your loved ones with you, and be happy."

But then Poncet blew the whole plan: he mentioned it to Fares.

The two children were called in front of his throne. Fares, the Lord of the Sea, was so angry that he wasn't even sitting on it, but walked up and down, occasionally thumping it with his fly-whisk. Makeda stood to one side, holding back her tears.

"WHO are you to decide who is sent by the Emperor on a mission of honour? Who are you, girl, to decide that you can leave your mother childless? Will she not suffer enough at losing her son, without losing you too? And HOW DARE YOU speak to the Frank before speaking to your father?"

The worst thing was facing Makeda afterwards. She sat on the bed in the dark hut with a child on each side of her, her arms around them, and at last said,

"I can't blame you. The future belongs to the young, and your future is to be together. If you want this badly enough, I'll help you."

Chapter 17

DISGUISED

The Big Rains had been over for two months now, but still Murad did not arrive. Doctor Poncet was beginning to fuss about "losing the monsoon", as he called it.

"If we don't leave soon, my child," he explained to Abraham, "there will be no wind to blow us north up the Red Sea."

Abraham and the doctor were sitting under the big tree outside the yard gate. Most days since he had arrived in Dibarwa, Poncet used to spend a bit of time telling the boy stories about France, which Abraham then passed on to Lahia and the other children. Today, as usual, Abraham begged,

"Teach me some more French, Doctor Poncet!"

Ethiopia: At Home

He knew the French words by now for all sorts of things and actions: "mother", "father", "sister", "lion", "like", "don't like", and so on, as well as some high-sounding whole sentences. It wasn't too hard, really, not for someone who already knew by heart more than forty of the 150 Psalms of David. He stood up, practised a couple of deep bows like a real Frank, the way Doctor Poncet had taught him, and then went through some of his lines:

"The Emperor of Ethiopia sends brotherly greetings to the King of the Franks!"

and

"My name is Abraham, and my father is a noble lord of Africa."

and

"France is a most beautiful and interesting country."

Today they had a go at greetings, and asking after people's health, but Doctor Poncet seemed distracted, and they stopped early.

Abraham Hannibal

Another week of waiting passed, and it was the night before the caravan was to leave for Massawa and the sea. They had given up waiting for Murad and the horses, and were just taking some bales of coffee-beans, perfume and spices to sell on the way, and small gifts like gold brooches and bracelets, as well as the ears and feet of the dead elephant (a funny kind of present for Louis, the Sun King, thought Abraham and Lahia). Granny Ester and the stepmothers were trying to comfort the nine children. Some of them were younger than Abraham, some were several years older, but all of them were anxious, lonely and scared.

Abraham was sitting in the hut with his mother and sister, and Makeda was trying, as well as she could in the dim light, to cut off the lovely black cloud of Lahia's hair.

"When your father asks where you are," she said to the girl, "I'll say that you are sick with grief and need to rest. By the time he discovers the truth, it'll be too late."

"He won't beat you, Mother, will he, when he finds out?" asked Abraham anxiously.

Ethiopia: At Home

Makeda shrugged. "And if he does? Come on. That's good enough now, Lahia. Let's change your clothes."

And Lahia put on a set of boy's clothes, very rough and poor - dirty white cotton breeches, shirt and cloak.

"Do I pass for a donkey-boy, now?"

She did. Abraham and Makeda would have laughed if they hadn't been feeling so tense.

It was no good trying to sleep. They talked about Nimrod, and how Makeda would look after him and make sure he didn't miss them too much; Abraham told them, yet again, Doctor Poncet's stories of France and the Sun King; and they talked about how one day they would come back to Dibarwa, grown-up and full of knowledge of the world.

Then, at last, they could hear people beginning to stir, and they said a last goodbye to Makeda inside the hut, for Lahia was to slip down into town under cover of darkness, and join the caravan there.

The three of them hugged each other tightly, tightly, sitting on the clay bed in the darkness of the hut.

"You'll always have each other," whispered Makeda. "You are mother and father to each other now, mother and father."

They all smiled, and she wiped the tears from her eyes and theirs with a corner of her white cloak.

Abraham went out to where Nimrod lay chained in the yard, and he knelt on the dusty ground and buried his face in Nimrod's great rough mane.

"Oh Nimrod, my lion, my lion! I thought you would be my lion for ever! Oh, my lion, Nimrod!"

And he rubbed Nimrod's big soft ears and tickled him under his chin for the last time, and Nimrod growled gently, as if he knew.

Then Abba Mikail came and blessed the travellers and their journey, and checked that Abraham was still wearing the little silver cross that he had received at his christening.

Finally, Abraham said goodbye to his father, and bowed and kissed his feet. His father raised him up, rested his hands on the

boy's shoulders, and said quietly,

"Remember, Abraham, our Emperor's words. Show the King of the Franks that the youth of Ethiopia is the best in the world for courage, wisdom, and high breeding. Show him."

But then the tall, stern-faced man picked him up and cuddled him as if he was still a tiny boy, and Abraham clung to him fiercely, but without a sound or a tear.

And as the stars faded and the sky grew pale, Makeda sat watching on the compound wall once again, this time facing north-east, towards the sea, and watched the caravan disappear out of sight. And this time, she knew, it was no use waiting for it to come back.

Chapter 18

DROWNED IN THE RED SEA

Abraham had never known heat like it, not even down in the valley of the Terrible River.

They had been picking their way for three days now down the vast, steep mountain-side that separates High Ethiopia from the coastal lowlands. With each step, the air was becoming heavier and wetter and hotter, and Abraham and the other highlanders weren't used to it; nor were the poor donkeys.

Doctor Poncet was having terrible trouble with his shoes - it was bad enough for the others with their nimble bare feet - but he had cheered everyone up by taking his hair off. Instead, he was wearing a huge straw hat.

Ethiopia: The Coast

Below they could see a sandy plain, dotted with trees. Then one of the old donkey-drivers shouted out,

"The sea! The sea!"

Far beyond was a hazy shimmer. The children all squinted at it through the sun, but it didn't really look like anything - unless you knew. Three days later they were standing sweltering next to it: an endless stretch of blue water, bigger than the children could ever have imagined.

"I can't believe we're going across *that*," muttered Abraham to Lahia, who was standing next to him with her cloak round her head, still in donkey-boy disguise. A few little gifts to the other donkey-boys had made sure that they didn't pass her secret to the caravan-leader and Doctor Poncet, and the nine other noble children had sworn to keep it too.

Doctor Poncet didn't seem to think much of the boats. He marched up and down the harbour-edge, shouting and waving his arms about.

"Look at these dhows! Not a nail in any of 'em anywhere! Planks tied together with *ropes*, for God's sake! And look at those monstrous sails! *Coconut-leaf mats*, would you believe it! Far too heavy and rough for the crew to move safely! And what about the mast? What are we supposed to do with a single mast if it breaks in a storm, eh? In any case, they're all far too small!"

In the end, he found an Indian-built boat with two masts and cotton sails instead of a local Arab dhow, and the cargo was loaded onto it. Now was the moment the two children had been dreading.

The load-bearers and the donkey-drivers, and all of the servants except for Doctor Poncet's two special ones, weren't needed any longer, and were about to be paid off and sent home. Lahia picked up a stray package, and she and Abraham and the other children walked steadily up the gang-plank on board the ship; then she pretended to be busy behind a pile of cargo in the hold.

Abraham watched Poncet paying the men on the shore and saying goodbye. The line of men in front of him was moving oh-so-slowly, but at last there were only two left.

Ethiopia: The Coast

"We'll be leaving soon, I think!" he hissed at Lahia.

But suddenly the ship's mate came past her, stopped, and pulled her up on deck.

"Don't forget this one," he shouted across at the caravan-leader.

The caravan-leader squinted at her across the fierce sunlight and called,

"Come on, boy! We're all off home now!"

Lahia grabbed hold of a piece of the rigging and shouted back,

"I'm not going home! I'm going with the ship!"

The caravan-leader looked at Doctor Poncet in bewilderment and started to explain the delay to him as best he could; Abraham dashed to the ship's side and called to him,

"Come here, sir, if you please. Come right on board."

The puzzled doctor did as he was asked.

"Doctor Poncet, that's my sister. You know how much she wants to come with me - how much I want her to come."

"But your father has forbidden it."

"My mother knows. She helped us."

The doctor sighed. "I don't know. What will your father say?"

"You'll never see him again. *Please,* Doctor Poncet."

And Lahia called across from where she was clinging on to the ship's rigging.

"*Please,* Doctor Poncet."

"Oh, very well. Come with us."

And he clumped back down to the harbour and told the caravan-leader,

"She ... he ... isn't one of yours. He's coming with us."

The morning wore on, and the sticky heat was becoming unbearable. Dr Poncet bustled around the harbour and the boat, back and forth across the gang-plank, getting pinker and shinier every minute.

"Dr Poncet, why don't you have a swim in the sea to cool down?" said Abraham, innocently.

Doctor Poncet gave him a hard look.

"It's salt water, don't you know? It just

makes you sticky. Besides, I can't swim. But you go ahead. We're not setting sail for a while."

Abraham looked down at the sparkling blue water below the ship's sides. It was so clear that he could see tiny stones on the bottom, some fifteen or twenty feet below, and great flocks of bright little fish darting this way and that.

He shook his head. "No, thanks. I can't swim either."

Instead, Abraham and the other children practised walking across the deck; although the sea was calm, they could feel the roll of the waves, and the little ship rocking beneath their feet - a strange, unbalancing sort of feeling.

Finally, the doctor was back on board after paying everyone off, the cargo was stowed, the crew were hoisting the sails, and by now Abraham and Lahia were too excited to be sad. The caravan-men were sitting in the shade watching, waiting to wave goodbye before going off and spending their money.

Suddenly there was a commotion over

by the harbour-entrance. Two men, travel-stained and panting, came running across and called to the caravan-men,

"Is that the Frankish doctor's ship?"

They barely waited for a reply, but raced across the gang-plank and on board the ship. They were two men from Fares's court.

"Where's Lahia?"

But Lahia had already jumped down into the cargo-hold and was crouching behind a sack of coffee-beans.

"Lahia!" called one. "Your father commands you to come back. You will not be punished. Come here, wherever you are!"

One of the younger children suddenly burst into tears. The men strode over to him, squatted down at his face-level and asked again,

"Where is Lahia?"

The boy, sobbing, pointed down into the hold, and the men were down there in a few strides.

"Let me go! Let me go! I'm not going home! I'm not! I'm not! Let me go!"

They came up with Lahia wriggling and

lashing out between them.

"Listen, I have gold! I can give you gold! I have all my jewellery! Let me go with my brother!"

One of the men flung her over his shoulder, and they marched back to the shore. The other man picked up the flimsy gang-plank and threw it onto the ship, and started to untie the mooring-ropes, shouting,

"Go now! Set sail!"

The captain looked enquiringly at Doctor Poncet; the doctor shrugged.

"Yes, set sail."

Abraham stood at the ship's side and called at the two men, standing on each side of the girl, their arms firmly linked with hers.

"Don't take her yet! We haven't said goodbye! Lahia, don't be afraid for me! I'll be all right, I really will! Look after Mother. And one day I will come back. I promise I will. Goodbye, Lahia."

But Lahia just stood and sobbed, with terrible shaking, silent sobs.

Two sailors pushed the little ship off, the wind filled her sails, and she moved away from the harbour-side. The five girls and the other

Ethiopia: The Coast

four boys stood clutching each other, looking wildly back at the land they were leaving, but Abraham stood alone at the ship's stern, calling,

"Goodbye, Lahia. I'll never forget you! Goodbye!"

The two men relaxed their hold. Suddenly, Lahia broke free from them, and Abraham, with horror, saw her run to the water's edge with a cry of "Wait for me!", rip off her cloak, and plunge in. Her first strokes were strong; she splashed bravely against the waves; desperation drove her forward.

Abraham and the other children, Doctor Poncet, his servants and the crew stood as if turned to stone, staring. Not one of them could swim. But the captain started to bring the ship about, and Abraham called out,

"She's going to make it! She's going to make it! Keep going, Lahia! You're going to make it!"

And Fares's two men, in spite of themselves, *willed* her to reach the ship.

But it was no use. The ship was already too far from the dock. She swallowed water and choked, her arms and legs grew tired, she sank and struggled to the surface again. Abraham suddenly pulled off his cloak too, and started to clamber over the side of the boat.

I'm going in. So what if I can't really swim? At least I'm better at it than she is.

But Doctor Poncet grabbed him and pulled him back.

"No, my boy! No! There's no sense in two deaths."

And as Abraham stood panting in Doctor Poncet's grip, Lahia at last sank slowly down, down, down, beneath the dazzlingly clear blue waves.

Chapter 19

RAIDERS OF THE DESERT SANDS

The next weeks passed in a blur of sickness, heat, and misery. *Oh, Lahia! Why did you do it? And why didn't I save you? Oh, Lahia!*

But the endless sickness in Abraham's stomach did a little to make him forget the sickness in his heart. Doctor Poncet sat with him, hour after hour, putting wet cloths on his forehead, persuading him to eat.

From time to time they put ashore, at small islands on the way, or, as soon as they had crossed the Red Sea, at harbours all the way up the coast of Arabia. It was safest to sail only in daylight, for the best chance of spotting sandbanks and rocks, since the Red Sea is one of the most dangerous in the world, and so they would anchor every night at sundown. But whenever the crew went off for fresh water and supplies, Abraham just stayed on board, curled up on his cloak.

At last, when his stomach felt better, he sat all day by the side of the ship, endlessly looking back towards the coast of Africa, until the hot sun sank into the sea, and the pale stars rose in its place.

At last he had to leave the ship. They had arrived at the big port of Jedda on the coast of Arabia, and Doctor Poncet wanted to have one more try at waiting for the Emperor's special messenger, Murad. There were unexpected problems. Poncet's servants spent half a day looking for accommodation, and came back with long faces. Jedda was full up.

"Curse it!" cried the doctor, as they all sat in a coffee-house in the harbour. "Of course! It's the time of the Pilgrimage. It's the Feast of the Sacrifice soon. Your feast, Abraham, did you know that?" And he put his arm around the boy, for he was a soft-hearted man, and he was worried about him.

Abraham looked puzzled.

Poncet started explaining, "The Muslims celebrate the time when God asked Abraham, in the days of old, to sacrifice his son Isaac ..."

"... but in the end gave him a ram to sacrifice instead?" cut in Abraham. Of course, he knew the story well - it was "his" story.

"That's right. Well, at least once in their lifetime, Muslims are supposed to make a pilgrimage to the holy city of Mecca, at the time of the Feast of the Sacrifice. There must be thousands of them on their way there, or there already, from all over - India, Africa, Turkey ... by camel caravan or by ship. We're in the nearest port to Mecca, so that's why there's no room for us in the inn."

In the end, they did find somewhere, probably cooler and cleaner than the inns in the town: a camp of large tents on the outskirts of Jedda, put up as extra accommodation, with a special section for travellers like themselves who were not Muslims. Their area was known as "the Camp of the Franks", the Arabs' word for all Christians from the cold northern countries; the ten children, being so obviously not from the north, got some strange looks from the merchants staying there. Poncet, his servants, and the ten children settled in to wait. It was grim countryside, all bare pebbly desert and rocks, with not a blade of grass. Drinking-water cost a fortune, and so did fresh fruit and vegetables, which had to come all the way from the mountains. Still Murad didn't come.

But the waiting suddenly ended, in a horribly unexpected way.

Abraham was sleeping, as well as he could in the sticky heat. He dreamt that he and Lahia were running, running for dear life, away from some dreadful beast. Slowly he realised that the beast was Nimrod, but swollen to a huge size, bellowing like an elephant, and his paws drumming on the ground with the noise of thunder. He woke up, his stomach cold with panic, and could dimly see Doctor Poncet standing in the middle of the tent, his white night-shirt glimmering in the half-light of dawn, and the other children jumping up wildly from their beds. There was a confused din of shouting and screaming, of camels braying, of feet pounding, of swords clashing. Then two men with drawn swords burst into the tent.

"Hand over all your money and valuables, and you won't be harmed!" shouted one, and then stopped and peered through the dark. "What's this? Hey! Men! In here! We have a whole nest of little slaves in here!"

"Th-they are not slaves," stammered Doctor Poncet. "They are n-noble youths of Ethiopia, on a mission to the King of France."

The man strode over to Poncet, gripped him by the shoulder, and pushed him onto the ground with a crash. Then the tent was suddenly full of men, and Abraham felt himself seized round the waist and carried off upside-down. Then he was outside the tent, and up on a camel's back, across the saddle,

and the rider was shouting something to the other raiders. And then his camel and about thirty others were lurching at tremendous speed across the stony desert.

Chapter 20

THE CROSS IN THE DUST

"I 've never seen anyone so ugly in my life," thought Abraham, as he and his friends, as well as twenty or so other prisoners from the camp, stood in front of a fine tent, their hands tied together in front of them. Doctor Poncet's ten children had managed to squirm their way next to each other and stood in a huddle, shoulder-to-shoulder, in spite of the heat - the sun was up now, and the chill of the desert night had long since worn off. A huge heap of bales and boxes that the raiders had stolen from the camp lay to one side.

A desert Arab in rich long robes was striding slowly up and down in front of his prisoners, looking them up and down with hard and calculating eyes. A long, curved dagger in a golden scabbard was stuck into his golden belt. His beard was grey, and wisps of grey hair stuck out from under the fine white cloth over his head. His skin was a sickly yellow colour, and his lower lip had a strange slit in it on the right hand side, so that from time to time spit dribbled out through it, which he dabbed at with a handkerchief.

"A good night's work, men! Well done! I will make my selection. Then take the rest to the market in Mecca and get them sold."

And he carried on his striding up and down, pointing at all of the girls in Doctor Poncet's group and the two biggest, strongest boys, as well as a dark sweet-faced girl and some strong-looking black boys that Abraham didn't know ... His men came and pulled them out from the crowd and took them to one side.

"Now, men!" barked the man with the slit slip. "Let's get all these pagan blacks to join the faithful! Get them lined up! My slaves first!"

The prisoners he had picked were

pushed into line and the first one, a boy, was made to stand in front of one the raiders. The leader stood back and watched. The raider grabbed the boy's chin in his hand and commanded,

"Repeat after me, 'There is no God but God, and Mohammed is his Prophet.'"

The boy clearly didn't understand a word he was saying, and just stared at him dumbly.

The raider slapped him round the face.

"REPEAT, you pagan dog! 'There is no God ...'"

The boy began to get the idea, and, stumbling and hesitating, repeated the words. The raider pushed him off to one side, and the next slave, a girl this time, came to the front. She stumbled out the words after him, and was pushed off in her turn. And so it went on, slave after slave.

"It's going to be our turn soon," muttered Abraham to the only two other children from his group who were still with him, Tadesse and Aferwerk, two boys both quite a bit older than him. He knew neither of them spoke Arabic.

"What's going on?" said Aferwerk. "What's everyone being made to say?"

"Don't you see?" exclaimed Abraham. "They're all being made to swear they believe in the Muslim God. Maybe most of them are just pagans, but we're being made to swear it too! Us Christians! We can't do that! We just can't!"

"I think all the others just have," said Tadesse, quite calmly. "But it's only words, isn't it? We don't have to believe it in our hearts."

"How can you *say* such a thing?" burst out Abraham fiercely. "That's ... that's ... *cheating*!"

"I don't think we have any choice," said Afewerk. But as he spoke, he and the other prisoners who hadn't been picked by the man with the slit lip were pushed into line.

Afewerk was number seven, and with just a quick sideways glance at Abraham, he repeated the words.

Tadesse was number nine, and he repeated the oath too, looking down at his feet. Then came a girl, and finally Abraham,

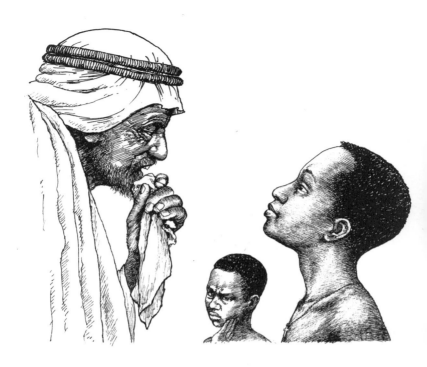

speaking a clear, confident Arabic. He knew now what he was going to say.

"There is no God but God, and Mohammed is his Prophet. And Jesus Christ is the Son of God, and Mary is his mother."

The raider in charge stared at him.

"*WHAT* did you say?"

Abraham stared straight back in the man's face, and repeated what he had said. Without exactly meaning to, he lifted his two hands, still tied together at the wrist, up to the silver cross he wore on a string round his neck, and held it out. As he spoke this time, his voice wobbled - he couldn't help it. The Arab lifted his hand to strike,

"You dog! You Christian ... "

But the voice of the man with the slit lip rang out, "STOP!" With a few quick strides he was standing next to them.

"Move away, Kemal," he said to the guard. "This boy interests me."

He looked Abraham up and down. "So you are a Christian, little boy! And how is it that a black like you doesn't worship sticks and stones?"

"I am from Ethiopia, the land of Christians. I worship one God, just like you" said Abraham, firmly. "I am of the line of Solomon, King of the Jews."

"Hmmm ..." muttered the Arab with the slit lip. "So you really are one of the children of the Holy Book ... And an Ethiopian, too, though you don't look like one ... Our Prophet Mohammed had a soft spot for the Ethiopians, you know, ever since they welcomed him in his hour of need. You have courage. I like that. I shall overlook your ...

your ... outburst. In fact, I have a mind not to sell you after all, and keep you here instead."

He dabbed at the spit on his chin for a moment. "On second thoughts, perhaps you'd be a bit of a trouble-maker. You can go and do that somewhere else. And keep that Christian cross of yours well hidden! Men! Take these prisoners off to the slave-market!"

And as the little group was gathered together, to be given water and some dry flat bread, Abraham suddenly found that he was shaking all over with a great rush of delayed fear, dizzy and sick and deathly cold in his stomach. He drank the water – it was awkward, holding the cup with his hands tied - but felt too sick for the bread, though he had the sense to tuck it inside his clothes for later.

So, as the sun grew higher and its heat fiercer, Abraham's group, including Afewerk and Tadesse, were formed into a line and marched off along the desert track to Mecca, their guards trotting up and down along the little caravan on their camels. To Abraham's dismay, he saw that Kemal, the guard who had nearly struck him, was one of them.

Arabia

Kemal ... Kemal ...one of our Muslim merchants at home was called that too ... what a monster this one is ... you wouldn't catch THIS Kemal giving beads away, being kind to Christian children ...

He could see Lahia now, wearing those five clear blue beads with the swirling red and yellow patterns inside them, smiling up at the other Kemal ...

It's better not to remember things.

As they marched, the hot sand burning its way even through the thick, hard soles of Abraham's feet, he noticed that one of the guards was as black-skinned as he was.

"Peace be with you!" he called up to the guard.

"And peace be with you! You speak good Arabic, boy!"

"Thank you. Are *you* an Arab, then?"

"I am a slave, as you are."

The words were said kindly, but they were like a slap across the face.

A slave ... Yes, that's what I am now ... When I left home, I was the Emperor's special messenger to the King of the Franks, I was the son of a Prince ...

... And now I'm a slave ...

The cold and the dizziness seized him again. Hardly knowing what he was saying, he mumbled,

"How did *you* come to be a slave?"

"When I was a child, in the Land of the Black People, I was out herding the cattle one day, and raiders caught me and carried me off to the sea. I was brought to Jedda, and sold to the King."

"The King?" asked Abraham, confused. The only kings he could think of were the Emperor Jesus the Great at Gondar, and the King of the Franks.

"You saw him just now, at his camp."

Without thinking, Abraham touched the right side of his mouth.

The guard went on, "That's right. The one with the slit in his lip. He is the King of Mecca, but he loves nothing more than to live in the desert, and do battle with his enemies, and raid the caravans that come for the Pilgrimage. Your friends who were chosen by him are now his slaves."

"What ... what will become of the rest of us now?"

Arabia

"Well, at this time of the year, there are plenty of merchants who have come from far and wide to make the Pilgrimage, and buy and sell at the Pilgrimage Market while they are here. You could be bought by a merchant from anywhere, and taken back to his land. What's your name, by the way?"

"Abraham."

"Abraham? Oh, of course, we call him *Ibrahim.* It is your feast very soon! My name is Saeed. But it is too hot for walking now. We must rest."

The path was full of pilgrims making their way towards the Holy City, and a pilgrims' rest house was just ahead of them, a jumble of dried mud buildings and the long black tents of the desert Arabs. The children and their guards washed and then ate and rested in one of the tents.

And then, as Abraham, desperately tired, but too tired to sleep, lay in the hot shade, he couldn't help remembering …

Oh, Granny, you always said to mind out for kidnappers … I did mind out, and now it's happened anyway … I belong to someone else now, someone I don't even know ... And I'll never see home again, or Mother or Father ... and there's Lahia, drowned because of me ... and dear funny Doctor Poncet - I don't even know if he's dead or alive ...

Suddenly, the pain of losing them all seemed too much to bear, and he started to sob, so hard that it hurt his whole body. Tadesse and Afewerk came and stroked him with their bound hands, and Afewerk whispered,

"Abraham, how can *you* cry? *You're* the strong one, you're the one who always knows what to do. Don't give up. Just think, at least we're still alive."

"I don't think I want to be alive. Not if it's going to be like this." And he sobbed still more wildly. "My mother's song ... when it says 'they leave us alone in strange hands' ...D'you think our slaves at home felt like this? ... I never thought about it ... "

Tadesse and Afewerk looked at each other in bewilderment.

"What is it, Abraham? What are you talking about? What song?"

"The Kunama, the Slave-People ... our

slaves at home ... I always thought they were happy ... I mean, we played together ... it was just normal ... but they were taken from their homes too ... they had to belong to my father ..."

And, choking and sobbing, Abraham gasped out his mother's song of the children of the Slave-People,

"They come and catch us by the waters of
the Mareb,
They make us slaves.
Our mothers in fear flee to the
mountains,
And leave us alone in strange hands ..."

"...They were in strange hands, and now we are too ... and ... and ... and ... I'll never see my mother again ..."

And Abraham sobbed and sobbed, for himself and for the slaves at home, and for everything that he would never see again.

Kemal suddenly strode over, grabbed the cross round Abraham's neck, and jerked him up off the ground so that the string cut into his flesh. He pulled his dagger out from its sheath; Abraham could feel the broad, curved blade cold against his neck, even in this heat. The knife slid under the string, which suddenly snapped, and Kemal took the cross in his hand. He looked at it, and spat.

"Well, we're not going to keep this, are we?"

He strode to the edge of the tent and flung the cross in a great spinning arc far into the desert. Abraham stood, staring wordlessly, his tears shocked out of him.

I've worn that cross since I was a baby. It's part of me …

Kemal strode back, and laughed in his face.

"Not happy, are we, little monkey? I thought little monkeys liked playing! How about a bit of a monkey song-and-dance, then?"

Abraham simply stood and stared at him.

"*DANCE*, monkey! Or sing something! Sing something in monkey-language!"

Everyone was completely still, staring. Then Saeed took Kemal by the arm and said, quietly, "Come on. Leave him alone. It's getting cooler. Time to get on with the journey."

Kemal glared at him, and then shrugged.

"All right. Time to get on with the journey."

And so the last little piece of Ethiopia and the old life that Abraham had brought with him lay gleaming among the pebbles of the desert, until, in a little while, the hot wind buried it in dust and grit ...

And as Abraham trudged along the path, up into the bare stony hills, bits of one of the Psalms of David that he had learnt for Abba Mikail started floating into his mind, until in the end he remembered the part that he wanted,

"By the rivers of Babylon, there we sat
down,
Yea, we wept, when we remembered
Zion.
We hanged our harps upon the willows
in the midst thereof.
For there, they that carried us away captive
Required of us a song;

Abraham Hannibal

And they that wasted us, required of us
                                    mirth,
Saying, Sing us one of the songs of Zion.
How shall we sing the Lord's song in a
                              strange land?"

And Abraham remembered another Zion that he had seen at his father's side, a Zion in the land of Sheba, in Queen Makeda's country; and then he thought of his father's words to the Emperor,

"Grandmothers by the fireside are already telling stories of his deeds."

I won't give up hope ... I won't give up hope ... Maybe I am a slave, but you won't be ashamed of me, Father. Somehow, I'll get to France after all. Lahia, you always said that if you want something badly enough, and don't give up wanting it, you'll get it in the end. I won't be a slave for ever ... I WILL get free, and I WILL get to France. I'll get my message to the Sun King, I'll make sure of that. I'll show him that the youth of Ethiopia are the best in the world for wisdom and courage and high breeding, just as the Emperor said ...

Arabia

And then, very firmly, as he trudged across the hot pebbly desert of Arabia, he said aloud two of his French sentences,

"My name is Abraham, and my father is a noble lord of Africa. The Emperor of Ethiopia sends brotherly greetings to the King of the Franks."

Chapter 21

SOLD INTO SLAVERY

There followed long months when, time and time again, Abraham nearly did give up hope. There was the slave-market by the Great Mosque at Mecca, where would-be buyers peered at his teeth and his tongue and poked his ribs, and at last a skinny old Turkish merchant called Ahmet bought him and a stock of other slaves and took him away from Tadesse and Afewerk, the last two links with his home. And, as Abraham was led off by his new master, he thought,

I could belong to this man for the rest of my life … under orders for ever, like a mule or a plough-ox … That's how he looks at me, as if I was his mule or his ox …I wonder if Father's slaves felt like this

when they were captured ... I suppose we never talked about it ...

Then there were the forty days and nights of trudging up the stony Arabian desert with the long, slow Egyptian caravan of some twenty thousand camels, trudging through the night because of the unbearable heat of the day, trudging by the light of flaming wood-lamps carried on the top of tall poles, until as the morning sun began to bake the air and the sand beneath their feet, they stopped and made camp and ate and slept and at last, with the cooling of the day, reloaded the camels and set off again through the night.

And five times a day, the whole caravan stopped, whatever the heat, and turned to pray in the direction they had come from, the direction of Mecca; and Abraham knelt, and bowed, and stood up together with Master Ahmet and the thousands upon thousands of believers.

It was all those thousands of believers who wore down his courage, the courage that had made him stand up to Kemal and the King of Mecca: it seemed ridiculous even to try be the odd one out. But the prayers that *he* said, under his breath, were the prayers that his mother and Abba Mikail had taught him - the prayers of the Christians.

Abraham never felt easy in his mind during those times of prayer: it *did* seem like cheating, every time he bowed down towards Mecca ...

Bit-by-bit, I'm turning into somebody else ... my real life's slipping further and further away from me ... so is my real home ... something got lost forever with my little silver cross ... I'm not ME any more ...

And one thought was always at the front of his mind:

I have to get away from Master Ahmet ... I have to get free ... then no one can make me do this, ever again ... I WILL get to France, and deliver my message to the Sun King ...

And every time they made camp and he lay down to sleep, Abraham whispered to himself, like a magic charm, the words of his message to the King of the Franks ...

Abraham Hannibal

At last the deserts of Arabia ended, but then there was the long steep mountainside as they rounded the north of the Red Sea, where the camels died of exhaustion in their hundreds, and then the terrifying wastes of Sinai, where the path leads between sheer mountains of bare rock, trembling with heat.

All these weeks, Abraham was shooting up, growing taller and taller (although the food was poor), and thinner and older in the face, stronger in the legs. But there was no one who knew him to notice the change, no one to say, as his father always used to say when he came home after a long journey, "By Saint George, Abraham, you've grown! You'll be as tall as me in no time."

His father's joke, when he was in a good mood, was to pick Abraham up and hold him so that the boy's head was level with his own. "Look, Abraham! You're as tall as me already!" But here in the desert he was just any black slave, one of hundreds, and nobody knew him. Even his name had changed: he wasn't Abraham any more, but had to answer to the Muslim way of saying his name, *Ibrahim.*

Arabia and Egypt

At last there was green again, the wheat and cotton-fields by the River Nile. But soon there was the terror of Cairo, a city a hundred times bigger and busier than any Abraham had ever seen, where his master Ahmet had business selling and buying. Oh, the noise, the stink, the donkeys and horse-carts and camels, the numberless huge houses and endless narrow, twisting streets! The fear of getting lost, of being run down by a cart! And always having to rush between markets and inns, tea-houses and the riverside, taking messages and delivering packages, always bony, wrinkled Master Ahmet whining at him, his little grey beard waggling,

"Don't you understand anything, Ibrahim, you fool!" "What took you so long, Ibrahim?" "What d'you mean, you couldn't find the place, Ibrahim?"

Very soon a thought tempted him, but not for long …

I could just slip off, down one of these alleyways, and Master Ahmet would never find me …

But what's the use? How could I ever reach the land of the Franks – or get home? Imagine a black boy on the loose who can't account for himself!

Abraham Hannibal

I'd be arrested in no time!

Then there was a boat down the Nile to Alexandria on the sea-coast, where Master Ahmet hired a Turkish ship to load his cargo - wheat and dried fruit, cotton and coffee, silk, perfume and humans - and carry it to Istanbul. The goods and the grown-up slaves were packed down in the cargo-hold, but Abraham and the other slave-children just had their wrists tied together and were allowed to stay on deck.

They had to wait four days for the right wind, and then the ship sailed out past the old castle that guards the harbour of Alexandria, and into the blue of the Mediterranean Sea, stained with the mud that the Nile has carried so many thousand miles from the mountains of Ethiopia. And Abraham looked back at the land he was leaving, and looked at Africa for the last time.

But that ship was never to reach Istanbul.

Chapter 22

SHIPWRECK!

After three days they reached the island of Cyprus, where they stopped to fill up with fresh water and food, and then they carried on north-west. The slave-children had their wrists untied, except when they were in a port, and Abraham was almost beginning to enjoy himself. Flying fish and other, even stranger, sea-creatures leapt through the glittering blue water - dolphins was their name, he learnt. Some days there was no wind to speak of, and the little ship just bobbed with the waves, while other days a cool breeze blew, but it was never so rough that he felt sick.

The Turkish sailors were good-humoured, and he even made friends: there

Abraham Hannibal

was a little group of slave-children, as black as he was, but taller and thinner and with strange scars on their foreheads, who had been brought to the Cairo slave-market all the way down the Nile from deep in the Land of the Black People. Abraham and they couldn't understand each others' own languages, but the others had all learnt a fair bit of Arabic on the year's journey from their homeland, so they managed in that.

The slave-children scratched board games on the deck with charcoal, and played with any bits and pieces they could find, or played "Spot the dolphin" and "Count the flying fish", and Abraham would forget that he had a master now, that he had lost everything that was precious to him.

But at night, settling onto his mat in the crammed and stinking hold, he would whisper, like a magic charm, the words that somehow, sometime, he would say to the King of the Franks …

Abraham Hannibal

Then, very early on the nineteenth day, as they passed the first of the Greek islands, the sky that had been a peaceful blue since they left Africa turned grey and wild; the sea began to pitch and heave, and the wind blew in violent gusts. The sailors hastily lowered the sails, but the steersman could do nothing with the ship as she was driven on helplessly before the wind, rolling and plunging into the deep trough of one wave, tossed high on the crest of the next.

Screaming prayers and promises to be better people, the free passengers scrambled below decks to join the slaves down in the hold, but Abraham had other ideas, and began to struggle his way across the deck to the ship's side. His white cotton robe, heavy with water, wrapped itself tight around his legs, and the driving spears of rain stung his cheeks and his eyes. He could hardly stand upright against the force of the wind that tried to push him back with every slithering step he took, and whipped his face raw.

The deck, awash with rain and sea, pitched and tilted under Abraham's bare feet:

The Mediterranean Sea

one moment the ship's bows plunged down into the frothing grey sea, and as she was flung back again, water poured over her deck from the front. The next moment her bows were pointing skywards and her stern was in the water, and then she was hurled bows down again, water pouring over her deck from the back.

The din was horrific – the wind roaring, the rain hammering, every rope and plank and joint groaning, sailors yelling orders and curses, passengers and slaves screaming, and over and over again, great rumbling rolls of thunder from the storm-clouds above.

At last, Abraham reached the ship's side and clung on tight to the clammy wood. All around was nothing but an emptiness of grey – grey clouds, grey sea, merging one into the other, and the white of the huge waves breaking over the little ship ... and yet, Abraham was suddenly seized with a wild excitement.

This storm is the most powerful thing I've ever known! Like the time I rode Father's stallion, but far faster, far stronger! There's no Master Ahmet now –

no masters and no slaves. What can he do against this storm? Maybe we'll be driven onto land somewhere, and I'll escape. The Greek people are Christians, like Yanni – maybe they'll help me, and I'll get the land of the Franks after all. Oh, Lahia, help me to be as brave as you were!

Then the wild movement stopped with a fearful crash and judder. One of the masts snapped with a huge cracking sound, and toppled over with a great splintering of wood and ripping of ropes and canvas. For a moment there was a terrible stillness, and they knew that they had struck a rock.

The passengers and the slaves struggled up out onto the deck, and there was a wild rush and panic as the free passengers and the crew struggled in the stinging rain and roaring wind to get a place on the two little life-boats. Then, all at once, some of the sailors started shouting,

"LAND AHOY! LAND AHOY!"

The slaves knew they had no chance of being allowed a place in the crowded little boats, and they clung to the ship in despair, but Abraham called out,

The Mediterranean Sea

"Come on! Land's so near! The waves'll carry you there! Grab something that floats and JUMP!"

And he picked up a wooden hen-coop that had survived the storm, emptied out the chickens, and jumped with it into the boiling grey sea. He felt the water close over his head as he sank down and down into the darkness; then he found himself forced upwards again until his head was up out of the water, and he was sneezing and breathing in air once more.

Gripping his hen-coop, he struck out with his spare arm and his feet towards land. Bobbing in the water around him, he could see a few dark heads of slaves who had followed his example, but then the waves picked him up and hurled him away, plunged him deep down and tossed him up again, until, after a lifetime of battering and pitching, he at last felt himself scrape against the gravelly bottom, and staggered up out of the water and collapsed onto solid - though not very dry - land.

Chapter 23

THE ISLAND

The rain had stopped, and the afternoon sun was feebly trying to shine from between the clouds. They were inside a small natural harbour, and the sea was calmer here. From where Abraham was sitting, on the hill-side high up above the beach, he could see Ahmet the merchant striding up and down the water's edge like a madman, his wet robes flapping heavily against his thin body. "I am ruined, ruined! It's all lost! It's all lost!" came the thin sound of his voice, over and over again.

It was true. They could see the ship outside the little harbour, slanting wildly against the rock that had gashed her, the waves out in the open sea still battering her. She would not last long. Only one of the two life-boats had reached the shore, and the beach was dotted with sailors and passengers weeping, comforting each other, desperately looking out to sea and along the shore for those who had disappeared. But Abraham sat on the hill-side above the beach, away from the free survivors. One person only was with him, the only other slave still alive, and together they looked silently out at the sea.

There were over thirty slaves crammed on that boat, and now there's only the two of us left ... only two of us who had the luck to make it through that little gap in the rocks ...

"I just keep having to say goodbye," said Abraham at last. "It's always goodbye."

The other slave, Nagonga, was a very tall, thin, dark girl with short hair, and the straight, narrow scars of her people in rows across her forehead. She was a bit older than Abraham, and they had become quite friendly on the voyage. It wasn't that she looked or sounded like Lahia, but there was something about her that was calming and comforting, just the way his sister had been.

The Mediterranean: The Island

"For me also, it's always goodbye, goodbye, goodbye" replied Nagonga. "And soon maybe I will say goodbye to you also."

"STOP IT!" said Abraham. "It's no good thinking about it. Look, let's see what this land is like - Master Ahmet can't stop us. Maybe we can escape altogether!"

They scrambled up the steep wooded hill behind the beach and looked all around them. But there was no land to escape into. They were on a tiny island, with sheer rock cliffs on three sides, the harbour and beach on the fourth, and nothing but coarse grass, bushes, trees and - surprisingly, for an uninhabited island - a few dozen goats. Over towards where the evening sun was beginning to redden the sky was the dim smudge of a much larger island. But how to reach it?

There was at least a tiny stream flowing down the hillside towards the sea, and the children drank thankfully from that. Far down below, they could see the other survivors, some of them collapsed in huddles, others walking around purposefully, as if searching for something.

Abraham Hannibal

"Master Ahmet and the other people need water too," said Nagonga.

"You mean, you're worried they'll come here to look for it? I hope they'll find where the water flows down at the bottom of the hill. But we all need food. There are these goats, but how can we kill them? I don't have a knife. Do you?"

Nagonga shook her head. "I think we go back to the beach. How can we live here?"

"How can we live *there*? Nagonga, down there we have a master, we are slaves. Up here, there is only us. We can be free. Let's stay one night. Please."

A little later, some of the men from the ship came clambering up the hillside and looked around, just as the children had done; but it was an easy matter to hide in a clump of bushes, and soon the men went away. And, best of all, as they lay hiding, they saw a nanny-goat grazing nearby ... and ... FOOD! Her udder was stretched big and tight with milk. The two children looked at each other and grinned.

"I catch goat and you milk goat?" asked

Nagonga in a whisper. "Or you catch goat and I milk goat?"

"We'll have to take it in turns, I think," said Abraham. "We don't have a pot. I'll hold her first, and you drink. We can try and catch her together. Ready?"

The two children leapt out from behind the bush and threw themselves at the goat; then Abraham held it round the fore-quarters with one arm, grabbed its back legs with his other hand, and Nagonga lay on her back, wriggled under its belly and milked it straight into her mouth. The goat jumped and bleated like a mad thing, and Nagonga started off by getting a milk face-wash; it wasn't made easier by the fact that she got a fit of the giggles, and then that started Abraham off too.

At last both the goat and the children quietened down, and Nagonga got a long, warm, satisfying drink, and then she and Abraham changed places. It was an encouraging start.

That night, their stomachs full of warm goat's milk, they slept on beds of sweet-smelling twigs. But Abraham lay awake a long while first, looking up at the bright stars, the new stars of the north that he had never known at home.

This is like New Year and Christmas and Easter all rolled into one! The first day since Jedda that I'm my own master!

Chapter 24

GOAT ISLAND EXPLORED

The next day they breakfasted on milk, and watched the people milling around on the beach below. They watched a group of sailors launch the life-boat, and the survivors of the wreck crowded into it with a lot of fussing and splashing and arguing, and headed off towards the distant island, Master Ahmet included. Nagonga and Abraham, looked at each other in delight.

"We're free!"

Then the same thought struck both of them. Free to do what? Free to live on water and goat's milk on a tiny island for the rest of their lives? Free never to see another human face again?

"A ship will come," said Abraham, firmly. "A friendly ship. This is a safe harbour, with fresh water. I think a lot of people must know about it."

"Or it will be a ship of slaves, like Master Ahmet's," answered Nagonga. "We will go from the crocodile's teeth into the lion's claws."

With a stab of longing, Abraham suddenly thought of Nimrod. It was terrible, but his memories of the old days were getting fainter, and sometimes a whole day could pass and he wouldn't think of home, even though he always meant to. He grabbed Nagonga's arm.

"Come on, Nagonga! Let's explore our island! We're the masters here! Let's explore every inch! Who knows what we'll find! We can start by giving it a name. What shall we call it?"

Nagonga considered.

"Well ... I think these goats will save our lives. We can call it Goat Island."

"Why not ... in honour of them! Come

on! Let's explore Goat Island!" It took longer than they expected, though there was nothing very special to see until, as the sun was getting to its highest, they found, tucked inside the shade of a clump of trees, a tumbledown little cottage.

"No one's living in *there*," commented Abraham. "And no one's lived in there for a while."

The windows were so small and high that even Nagonga couldn't see in through them, and they crept in through the cracked wooden door, half-fearful of what they would find.

The cottage was very dark. It still had some rough furniture, as well as some strange wooden tubs. They went and peered inside them: they were thick with a whitish scum.

"Sour milk!" said Abraham, sniffing for a minute or two. The smell was very faint, but it was just like the butter-making pots at home when they'd been left too long without washing.

But Nagonga wasn't listening. She was staring at the bed. It had nothing on it but a thin straw-stuffed mattress, and right across it was a huge, faded stain.

"I think this is blood, Abraham."

"What? Where?"

Nagonga pointed silently. The two children stared at the stain.

"Maybe," said Nagonga quietly, "that is why the house is empty ... Enemies kill this man. And maybe people are afraid to live in the house now."

Without further discussion, the children tumbled out of the dark little house. They crashed through the trees as quickly as they could, and ran out up the sunny slopes, right into the middle of some startled goats.

"Nagonga," panted Abraham. "I think the man was the goat-herd. That is why the goats are alone on the island. People are afraid to live on this island, not just in the house."

"They must only be afraid if they think the killers will come back," said Nagonga, slowly. "You think they will come back?"

"Let's say they *won't* come back, but we'll make sure we keep a good look-out in case they do," answered Abraham.

The Mediterranean: The Island

And so, with this confusing advice, the children settled in on the island, to wait for whoever might arrive.

Chapter 25

THE LILY-FLOWER FLAG

The days passed. Abraham got a stick and scratched a mark on it for each day, just as he had done once before, on a journey long ago in a far-off land. The nanny-goats got quite used to being milked, though a liquid diet left the children permanently hungry.

Soon they began to brave the blood-stained cottage to use the pots for making soft cheese; Abraham ripped his robe into pieces to use as cheese-cloth, and lived in his under-shorts.

Neither Abraham nor Nagonga ever felt quite at ease. They would look anxiously out to

The Mediterranean: The Island

where the little harbour's mouth led to the open sea, not knowing whether to hope for a ship or not.

Three times they saw ships sail past, but they never changed course to come into the harbour. The children built themselves a little round hut of sticks and grass, and when they had done that, spent the time telling each other tales of their past lives, or - after a careful check out to sea - splashing in the shallow water near the beach. Neither of them ever tried swimming out of their depth ... deep water held too many memories, especially for Abraham ...

And every night, just as in the desert, just as on the ship, Abraham repeated to himself, like a magic charm, the words of his message to the Sun King.

Then, one day - Day 37 since the ship-wreck it was, by Abraham's stick - a ship did change course.

The children took no chances. They had

already found a perfect look-out spot, a huge cracked rock with bushes growing out of the cracks, high up on the slope overlooking the little harbour. They could stand behind it, shaded and hidden, and peer down onto the beach and the whole harbour, and that was what they did now.

The ship was a big one, almost too big for the tiny harbour, but it passed in through the narrow entrance skilfully. She was the biggest ship the children had ever seen, with two masts and at least ten sails, and shiny cannons poking out of her sides. As she came closer, they could see that she had had some kind of battering: there was the broken stump of a third mast, and the sails and rigging looked torn and untidy. But then, neither of them knew much about ships.

"Is it a slave-ship?" asked Nagonga. "I think the killers will come in a slave-ship."

"I wish I knew," whispered Abraham, not knowing why he was whispering, since the ship was far out of ear-shot. "But it looks quite different from Master Ahmet's one. I wonder if it's Frankish. That would be the best thing.

The Franks would never take a Christian as a slave."

There was a name written on the ship's side, but it was very far away, and in any case, Abraham had never learnt any of the Frankish or the Arabic alphabet.

"Don't forget I'm not a Christian," pointed out Nagonga.

"You're with me. You can *become* a Christian. Just like my mother, after she was captured."

There was a distant clank and rattle and splash, of the anchor-chain being lowered. The big ship was still quite far out, but it had come as near the shore as it dared. And then, as Abraham squinted at every corner of the ship, desperate for clues, a great flood of relief swept right through him. He gave a loud whoop of joy, pulled Nagonga out from behind the rock with both hands and whirled her round, chanting at the top of his voice,

"The lily-flower! The lily-flower! The lily-flower!"

The two of them whirled round and round until they both collapsed, breathless, on the grass. The goats that had been grazing nearby scattered in amazement. Nagonga was completely bewildered too.

"What's happened, Abraham? What *are* you saying?"

"Look! There! At the back of the ship! The ... the ... what d'you call it ... the *flag*! It's the lily-flower of France! D'you remember I told you about Doctor Poncet and the Sun King? It's their country! This ship will take us to France! To the Palace of the Sun King! I'm going to deliver my message at last! The Sun King is really going to see that the youth of Ethiopia are the best in the world! Second to nobody!"

Abraham knelt up and grabbed Nagonga by the shoulders, shouting into her face.

"Just think, Nagonga, just think! He'll be standing there, the Sun King'll be standing there in his Palace, in a huge hall with a hundred mirrors ... and each mirror is as tall as a tree ... there are enormous windows that look out over the Palace gardens ... there are stone images of animals and men out there, spouting water high into the air ... and trees and

Abraham Hannibal

bushes cut into amazing shapes ... and I'm in a carriage with wheels ... it's pulled by horses as fast as the wind, and I'm riding up the road through the gardens to the Sun King's Palace ... you're with me, of course, so we're both in the carriage, galloping nearer and nearer ... and when we get there, the servants help us to climb out of the carriage ... and there's music - drums and trumpets - to welcome us ... and the servants lead us up a gigantic staircase, with wonderful pictures painted on all the walls and the ceiling ... and the servants lead us into this enormous hall ... and there's the Sun King standing up on a platform, standing next to his huge, fancy golden chair ... he's wearing a bushy white wig just like Doctor Poncet, and shining clothes full of silver and gold thread, and a great cloak trimmed with fur ... his crown's on the table next to him ... and Doctor Poncet is there, smiling all over his face because he's *so* pleased to see that I've arrived at last ... and then I bow like a real Frank, like this,"

Abraham jumped to his feet, bowed low as the doctor had taught him all those months before, and shouted out at the top of his voice,

"The Emperor of Ethiopia sends brotherly greetings to the King of the Franks! My name is Abraham and my father is a noble lord of Africa!"

He pulled Nagonga to her feet.

"Come on, Nagonga! Let's go down and greet them!"

And hand-in-hand, the two children raced down the hillside to the beach, and waited for the Sun King's sailors.

AFTERWORD

Abraham was a real person. He himself wrote how his father was an African prince, and how he was taken from his home when he was a little boy. His family used to describe him weeping, as an old man, when he remembered his favourite sister drowning in the sea as his ship sailed away from the coast of Africa.

Some of the details of this story are made up, but many of the characters really existed: the Emperor Jesus the Great, Doctor Poncet, the King of Mecca (who really did kidnap Doctor Poncet's group of Ethiopian children), and of course, the Sun King, Louis the Fourteenth of France. Abraham really did get to France in the end, but he didn't spend his life there. He became a famous general and a rich land-owner in Russia (where he took the surname Hannibal). His great-grandson was the famous Russian writer Alexander Pushkin.

Read about Abraham's adventures after he escapes from Goat Island in "ABRAHAM HANNIBAL and the Battle for the Throne".

The Ethiopian Alphabet

On the opposite page you can see the alphabet that Abraham, like other Ethiopian children, had to learn – except that the full Ethiopian alphabet has even more letters – lots more!

Actually, the signs don't stand for single letters – they stand for whole syllables. For example, the sign for 'ha' (as in 'hat') is Ս, and there are different tiny changes to this sign for the other vowel sounds, like this:

Ս ha   Սᵘhoo   ℒhee   Ⴟhaa   Ⴟhey   Սhi   Ս'ho
(as in hat)(as in hoot)(as in heat)(as in hard)(as in hey!)(as in his)(as in horse)

So, for example, the name of Abraham's sister Lahia would look like this: ᎭᏌᎶ   Ꮤlaa   ℒhee   Ꮵya
Can you find all the signs on the chart opposite?

The name of his father Fares would look like this: ፈረስ   ፈfa   ፈrey   ስs (the little vowel after the 's' isn't pronounced) Can you find these signs too?

PUZZLE

See if you can use the chart opposite to read the words in the picture from The Stories of the Kings in chapter 3. The answers are at the end of the AUTHOR'S THANK YOU pages.

Try writing your names or your friends' names the Ethiopian way – or use the alphabet as your code for writing top-secret messages!

ሀ ha	ሁ hoo	ሂ hee	ሃ haa	ሄ hey	ህ hi	ሆ ho
ለ la	ሉ loo	ሊ lee	ላ laa	ሌ ley	ል li	ሎ lo
መ ma	ሙ moo	ሚ mee	ማ maa	ሜ mey	ም mi	ሞ mo
ሰ sa	ሱ soo	ሲ see	ሳ saa	ሴ sey	ስ si	ሶ so
ረ ra	ሩ roo	ሪ ree	ራ raa	ሬ rey	ር ri	ሮ ro
ሸ sha	ሹ shoo	ሺ shee	ሻ shaa	ሼ shey	ሽ shi	ሾ sho
በ ba	ቡ boo	ቢ bee	ባ baa	ቤ bey	ብ bi	ቦ bo
ጠ ta	ጡ too	ጢ tee	ጣ taa	ጤ tey	ጥ ti	ጦ to
ነ na	ኑ noo	ኒ nee	ና naa	ኔ ney	ን ni	ኖ no
አ a	ኡ oo	ኢ ee	ኣ aa	ኤ ey	እ i	ኦ o
ከ ka	ኩ koo	ኪ kee	ካ kaa	ኬ key	ክ ki	ኮ ko
ወ wa	ዉ woo	ዊ wee	ዋ waa	ዌ wey	ው wi	ዎ wo
ዘ za	ዙ zoo	ዚ zee	ዛ zaa	ዜ zey	ዝ zi	ዞ zo
የ ya	ዩ yoo	ዪ yee	ያ yaa	ዬ yey	ይ yi	ዮ yo
ደ da	ዱ doo	ዲ dee	ዳ daa	ዴ dey	ድ di	ዶ do
ጀ ja	ጁ joo	ጂ jee	ጃ jaa	ጄ jey	ጅ ji	ጆ jo
ገ ga	ጉ goo	ጊ gee	ጋ gaa	ጌ gey	ግ gi	ጎ go
ፈ fa	ፉ foo	ፊ fee	ፋ faa	ፌ fey	ፍ fi	ፎ fo
ፐ pa	ፑ poo	ፒ pee	ፓ paa	ፔ pey	ፕ pi	ፖ po

AUTHOR'S THANK YOU

I would like to thank everybody who helped to make this book happen. They are too many for me to mention them all, but here are some of them:

Stephen (Huey) Bell, for helping to look after our son, Abraham, while I was getting this book ready, for lending me his library of Ethiopian books, and for helping with the research

Eric Robson, my wonderful artist

Rita and Professor Richard Pankhurst, Assefa Gabre Mariam, Gabre Medhin and his family, Ato Mitiku and Ato Aforki, who all helped me in Ethiopia or Eritrea

Vera and Professor Leonid Arenshtein, Irina Yureva, Aysanew Kassa, Patrick Gilkes, Girma Ejere, Julian Kay, Aamir Ali, Professor Tony Briggs, and Tatiana Wolf, who all helped me in Russia or in England

Umberto Allemandi, John Aldridge, Lucy Bramley, Keith Gaines, Perilla Kinchin and Alastair Sawday, who all helped me with the publishing side of things

the adults and children who read and commented on the manuscript – Marilyn Malin, Chris McDonagh, Anna Somers Cocks, Peggy Somers Cocks, Susan Powell, Charlotte Rolfe, Martin Russell, Sue Rainey, Kate Canter, Andrew Thomas, Poppy Trevillion, Stefania Orlando, Geoffrey Howard, Emma Lloyd, Steven St Croix, Dean Flynn, Nellie Barrie, Fred Morgan, Jemima Bland, Shomari Charles, Stefan and Patrick Schrijnen, Katherine Hardy, Martha Paren.

Answers to Ethiopian Alphabet Puzzle

The words are:

Makeda, Solomon, Jerusalem.

SHORT BIBLIOGRAPHY

I researched Abraham's story and the background information as carefully and widely as I could. Here are some of the sources I used:

Manoel de ALMEIDA: *The History of High Ethiopia or Abassia* (edited by C.F. Beckingham and G.W. Huntingford, in *Some Records of Ethiopia, 1593 – 1646*; London, 1954)

James BRUCE: *Travels to Discover the Source of the Nile in the Years 1768, 1769, 1771, 1772 and 1773* (Edinburgh, 1790)

Georg LEETS: *Abraham Petrovich Hannibal, a biography* (published in Russian, Tallin, 1984)

Bernard LEWIS: *Race and Slavery in the Middle East* (New York, 1990)

Vladimir NABOKOV: introduction to his translation of *Eugene Onegin*, by Alexander Pushkin. (London, 1964)

Richard PANKHURST: *An Introduction to the Economic History of Ethiopia from Early Times to 1800* (London, 1961) and *A Social History of Ethiopia* (Addis Abeba, 1990); (editor) *The Ethiopian Royal Chronicles* (Nairobi, 1967)

Charles PONCET: *A Voyage to Aethiopia* Joseph PITTS: *A Faithful Account of the Religion and Manners of the Mahometans*; both reprinted by the Hakluyt Society (1949) under the title *The Red Sea and Adjacent Countries at the Close of the Seventeenth Century*

Henry SALT: *a Voyage to Abyssinia and Travels into the Interior of That Country* (London, 1814)

NOTE ON ABRAHAM'S COUNTRY OF BIRTH

All through this book, Abraham's country is referred to as Ethiopia. In fact, nowadays, much of the north-eastern part of Abraham's Ethiopia (including Dibarwa and Massawa) is a separate country called Eritrea. I have used the name Ethiopia in this book as it was the name used in Abraham's time for all the lands ruled by the Emperor in Gondar, including the lands ruled under him by the Lord of the Sea.

Read about Abraham's adventures after he escapes from Goat Island in

ABRAHAM HANNIBAL

and The Battle for the Throne

"If I want to do something badly enough, and don't give up, I'll do it in the end."

Abraham, the son of an Ethiopian prince, has been kidnapped and sold into slavery by the terrible Raiders of the Sands, while on a mission to the King of France. He survives shipwreck, only to be captured by pirates and sold again – to the Sultan of Turkey. He is smuggled out of the Sultan's vast and mysterious palace by agents of Peter, the Tsar of Russia, and becomes his most trusted page-boy. He wins freedom and fame on the battlefield – and at last achieves his mission.

Based on fact, this is the amazing story of a boy who went from slave to General in the Russian army – and became ancestor of a world-famous writer.

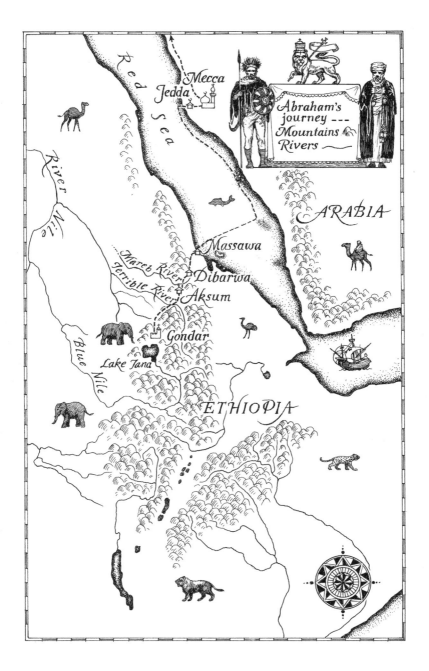

Red Sea

River Nile

Mecca

Jedda

ARABIA

Massawa

Mareb River

Terrible River

Dibarwa

Aksum

Blue Nile

Gondar

Lake Tana

ETHIOPIA

Abraham's
journey ---
Mountains
Rivers